T0289557

EXPLOSIONS

Michael Bay and the Pyrotechnics of the Imagination

Mathieu Poulin

EXPLOSIONS

Michael Bay and the Pyrotechnics
of the Imagination

Translated from the French by Aleshia Jensen

QC FICTION

Revision: Katherine Hastings
Proofreading: David Warriner, Elizabeth West
Book design: Folio infographie
Cover & logo: Maison 1608 by Solisco
Fiction editor: Peter McCambridge

Copyright © 2015 by Les Éditions de Ta Mère
Originally published as *Des explosions, ou Michael Bay et la pyrotechnie de l'esprit*
Translation Copyright © Aleshia Jensen

ISBN 978-1-77186-151-9 pbk; 978-1-77186-152-6 epub; 978-1-77186-153-3 pdf; 978-1-77186-154-0 mobi/pocket

Legal Deposit, 3rd quarter 2018
Bibliothèque et Archives nationales du Québec
Library and Archives Canada

Published by QC Fiction
6977, rue Lacroix
Montréal, Québec H4E 2V4
Telephone: 514 808-8504
QC@QCfiction.com
www.QCfiction.com

QC Fiction is an imprint of Baraka Books.

Printed and bound in Québec

Trade Distribution & Returns
Canada and the United States
Independent Publishers Group
1-800-888-4741
orders@ipgbook.com

We acknowledge the financial support of the Société de développement des entreprises culturelles (SODEC), the Government of Québec tax credit for book publishing administered by SODEC, the Government of Canada, and the Canada Council for the Arts.

Although inspired by real people, books, and movies, this story is a work of fiction.

ON THE DIFFICULTIES OF PILOTING A SPACE SHUTTLE THROUGH AN ASTEROID SHOWER

TRUTH'S WINDSHIELD exploded into a puzzle of seemingly incompatible fragments. The cabin pressure plunged. The pilot took one last glance at his family photo on the control panel and was sucked out into the vacuum of space, where he suffocated as his body expanded. A space rock the size of a baseball hurtled through the flight deck and effortlessly perforated the face of the co-pilot, who was still strapped in. A deafening blast of air swept through the cabin. Objects became dangerous projectiles. Behind the cockpit, crew members had just enough time to secure their helmets to their suits. While this did little to calm them, at least they could breathe.

Through his headset, Michael could only make out a word here or there amid a stream of orphaned syllables.

"*Tr*... Uston...Pl... Resp...What...Stat... *Tru*..."

The voice was insistent and panicked—far from reassuring. Michael's eyes were wide open, but it was hard to see through his foggy visor. The shuttle jackhammered and sent reverberations through his body. He felt sick to his stomach, but there was no time to indulge the thought. Around him, crew members not secured by seatbelts grasped for purchase as they fought the pull of the stars. Michael held fast to a colorful abstract painting with his left hand, preventing it from getting sucked up by the cosmos. His easel and brushes were already distant satellites in some unknown orbit.

Michael managed to turn to his right and saw *Independence* through the window. She was experiencing problems of her own. Debris from the asteroid hit one of the rear engines, which exploded into a fireball that was immediately extinguished by the void, as though someone had hit rewind. *Independence* was sent off course and into a tailspin.

Michael managed to pull the painting back toward him, stowed it in the compartment under his seat, and took out a video camera.

"*Uth*... Here... Pleas... Spond...Wh... Stat..."

Michael pressed the camera lens up to the window to capture a series of shaky but stunning images. *Independence* was flying erratically as she spun inside a comet's tail. Michael struggled to keep his shot in focus. Although the shooting schedule didn't account for such unique circumstances, Michael was determined to make the most of it. He'd find somewhere to fit in the spectacular shots—if he survived till post-production.

Something hard hit the back of his seat. The camera flew out of his hand, shot forward, and got lodged in an orange nylon net near the cockpit. Michael's seatbelt was still in place but, behind him, the astrophysicist's had given way. The scientist tried to grip the back of the seat, but his thick gloves and limited strength made it difficult to hold on. Feet appeared to the right of Michael's head, then, with another lurch of the shuttle, legs, pelvis, and torso. The astrophysicist's head was now right beside Michael's, but at a 90-degree angle. His body was straight as a board and he was clinging to the seatback with all his might, like a gymnast gripping a vertical bar, every muscle contracted, parallel to the ground. The two men locked eyes, then the scientist let go, flew across the shuttle, through the windshield, and became one with his object of study.

Michael tried to gather his wits. From the corner of his eye he could still see *Independence* on his right. There was something almost poetic about the distressed shuttle from afar. Her power and tragic beauty must clearly have been destined for his cinematic oeuvre. It would have been irresponsible to let the image slip away. Unable to reach the camera he'd dropped, Michael activated the hydraulic system and his seat moved on rails toward what was left of the main control panel. The buttons, controls, and displays still appeared to work.

"*Tru*... This... Respon... What I... Stat..."

Truth seemed to have stabilized. Up front, a crew member had managed to climb into the pilot's seat and, firmly buckled in, was more or less in control of the shuttle. Michael pressed a series of buttons and the back of the spacecraft groaned as it opened up. An enormous robotic arm emerged with three cameras attached. Drops of condensation obstructed the film-maker's view, but he continued to flip switches in a precise order. The monitors lit up. The cameras were on. Michael grabbed hold of the two controls and the robotic arm deftly extended. The first screen displayed an overhead shot of their shuttle's cockpit and nose, which looked like they'd been sprayed with bullets from guns of all calibers. The second panned out to follow *Independence* as she tailspinned and left a greyish trail behind her. On the third *Freedom* was clearly visible and seemingly intact. She slalomed in and out of the vapor trailing *Truth*. The mission's three vessels were in the frame. Without hesitating, Michael skillfully maneuvered the mechanical arm as it twirled and the shots came to life. Like his mind, the beautiful, frenetic images burst with kinetic energy.

Then the third monitor went to static. The asteroid fragments multiplied. The acting pilot seemed to have lost his composure. Michael looked up: the back of the seat had a gaping hole in it. The pilot's arms floated lifelessly. Another monitor lost its signal. Then an enormous shockwave rocked the shuttle, shunting it off course. Michael's neck whipped forward. His forehead hit the inside of his helmet. For a second everything was hazy, muffled. He didn't want to close his eyes. He didn't want to fall asleep. To his left, a man lay perfectly still, eyes contorted, mouth open, his beard frosted over, his visor shattered. Sparks flew from the control panel. Through the window, Michael watched part of the right wing float by.

"*Uth...* Please Respond... Rstat... *Truth...* Ouston..."

It was *Truth*'s turn to start spinning, first slowly, then faster and faster. Nobody seemed willing to take over the controls. The crew members still alive were petrified. Only Bruckheimer appeared stoic. Never one to give up easily, Michael took charge: he quickly scanned the space between him and the cockpit, and noted the potential obstacles and handholds. He checked his suit, closed his eyes, mentally embraced his beautiful PhD student, opened his eyes, then unclipped his belt. The pull was immediate. He crossed the length of the cabin in seconds, his body moving with the abandon of a rag doll thrown in front of a fighter-jet engine. He grabbed onto the orange nylon net as he passed it, slowing himself but, in the process, dislodging the camera, which flew out into the ether. The pilot's seat was a few feet away. The shuttle shook with increasing violence. Using his free hand, Michael grabbed one of the carabiners on his suit and clipped it to the net, praying it was firmly anchored to the wall. He leaned back and, his two hands now free, fixed a second carabiner to the seat back. He could see straight through the hole in the pilot's chest, which was covered with a thin film of frozen blood. *Truth* picked up speed as it rotated, like a bus rolling down a hill. Michael opened a pocket on his left thigh, pulled out a multipurpose blade and cut the length of

13

rope attaching him to the orange net so that he could get closer to the coveted seat. At the sight of the two perforated corpses, he could barely suppress the nausea rising in his throat. He concentrated, slowed his breathing, thought "I won't forget you, Corporal Witwicky," then undid the spaceman's harness and watched him instantly vanish through the windshield.

At the command station, Michael turned on the built-in microphone in his helmet.

"Houston, this is *Truth*. This is a distress call. Mayday. We've lost control. This is *Truth*. Houston, come in. Mayday."

The control panel was half singed, but the shuttle still responded—albeit feebly—to the steering commands. A few displays were still functional, including the Flight Director Attitude Indicator. Michael struggled to slow *Truth*'s spin and bring her nose up. An alarming number of rock fragments came into view. Farther out, to the right, he could see *Independence*. Her trajectory had changed dramatically. Their flight paths seemed set to cross and collision was imminent at their current speed. Michael pulled the controller toward him with all his might, but *Truth* barely responded. Amid millions of pieces of debris, the out-of-control shuttles zoomed toward each other. There seemed no way to avoid impact. Time seemed to have expanded, as if particularly sensitive to the laws of relativity. He stared at *Independence* as she continued to spin. Ten feet from the point of contact, one vessel was tail up and the other tail down. Their noses touched slightly. Michael and Ben Affleck exchanged a distressed look from their respective cockpits as the two shuttles brushed past one another at over twelve thousand miles per hour. A collision was narrowly avoided but, at that exact moment, an asteroid fragment struck *Independence*'s only functioning thruster. *Truth* reverberated and Michael saw nothing but flames. Everything went fuzzy. Was this the end? No, it couldn't be, not yet. He still had to win Daphné back. He still had to find the strength to patch things up with his parents. He still had to unravel the mystery of meaning.

He still had to become known to all as the greatest mind of the century.

ON THE DANGERS OF DRIVING A TANKER
TRUCK THROUGH RUSH HOUR TRAFFIC

THE FIRST RECORDED FACTS on Michael Bay date back to one fateful day in California history—March 19, 1967—dubbed "Fireball Sunday" by the following day's *Los Angeles Times*. At four in the afternoon, during a particularly grueling rush hour in the LA metropolitan area, a tanker transporting thirteen cubic feet of propane exploded out of the blue at the corner of East 1st Street and North Boyle Avenue, killing one hundred and seventy-two people instantly, wounding three hundred and fourteen, of whom one hundred and twenty-two subsequently succumbed to their burns, lacerations, and perforations. An enormously thick cloud of fire and smoke, which a number of veterans in the area confirmed not having "seen the likes of since Pearl Harbor," rose nine hundred and twenty-five feet up into the clear California spring sky, blasting away cars, passersby, windows, and debris—everything within a six hundred-foot radius. For the thirty seconds immediately following the explosion, nothing could be heard but the huge blazing ball's roar of victory and the piercing shrieks of car alarms. Then little by little yet growing more and more deafening, cries and angry shouts—some hoarse and high-pitched, others slick and muffled—sounded through the air, as the survivors who had not immediately lost consciousness suddenly, with the anesthetizing effect of the confusion wearing off, felt the full agony of their segmented limbs, their open wounds revealing organs burnt to a cinder, or finding their loved ones dead and beyond recognition. Those who escaped relatively unscathed were struck with waves of nausea at the sight of hundreds reduced to a vulgar pile of burnt corpses, coupled with the shock and revolting smell in the air (mostly propane, blood, smoke, and vomit, hitting the senses one at a time to form a whole that would forever be associated with chaos), giving way to numerous instances of regurgitation that left the scene completely devoid of poetic potential.

After the first confused minutes following the blast, which seemed unbearably long from the perspective of the crippled and widowers- and widows-to-be, the first emergency vehicles finally arrived at the scene. The Los Angeles Fire Department, assisted by numerous medics and city police officers, quickly realized it was woefully underequipped to handle the situation. All while the fire, which had first filled the sky with its majestic glow, now began spreading at ground level, devouring everything in its path, including objects no one would have thought flammable. Telephone poles weak from the blast collapsed one by one, their transformers exploding into fountains of sparks like Kerouac's roman candles. The gleam of the flames gradually became one with the immense orange sun setting over downtown in the City of Angels. On the horizon, a fleet of helicopters with blurred halos appeared against the smoldering sky, then landed on-site and emptied out marines, who were reassuring if only for their seemingly choreographed efficiency.

And amid it all, unharmed and observing the scene around him, a young boy stood all alone.

Laughing.

AT THE AGE OF 12, Michael Bay discovered Plato on one of his many afternoons at the Los Angeles Public Library and knew at once that he was destined to one day be a philosopher. After reading a wide variety of writers— from Dickens and Wilde to Desnos, Faulkner, Borgès, Robbe-Grillet, Aquin, Proust, Césaire, and Moravia— young Michael felt it was time to expand his horizons. So far as he was concerned, acquiring knowledge from books was the best way to lend meaning to his existence which, due to the haziness of his own history, was cruelly lacking in it.

It was this notion of origin that led him to Plato's works, his curiosity piqued by an article in *The Hollywood Reporter* titled "A Return to Plato for an Understanding of Today? Thoughts on Origin and Truth" by guest columnist Jerry Bruckheimer. Michael began researching a field vaster than fiction, to which he had always been partial. Out of habit, he turned to an old edition of the *Encyclopedia Britannica*, whose odor of paste and paper still imbues his memories today, and read the pages dedicated to the Greek philosopher with puzzled interest. Then, he walked over to a shelf and pulled down *Symposium* for the first time, his choice no doubt subconsciously motivated by its subtitle, *On Love*.

ON MEATLOAF

IN FEBRUARY 1993, following the release of the album *Bat Out of Hell II: Back into Hell,* Virgin Records contacted Michael Bay, at the request of Meat Loaf himself, to ask if he would meet with the musician in private to discuss a possible collaboration. Michael was enthusiastic about the idea, having played the role of Eddie in a theatrical homage to *The Rocky Horror Picture Show* and supervised its *mise en scène* in his freshman year at Wesleyan University. He accepted at once, if only out of curiosity. A meeting was set for cocktail hour in a trendy university bookstore-café where both men were regular customers. The cuisine was refined but not pretentious, and the décor understated and tasteful—particularly on the back patio, where thin slivers of light filtered through an elegant vine-covered trellis—and that same evening, the bookstore was set to host a round table discussion on destiny and metaphysics featuring Paul Auster, Jacques Derrida, Umberto Eco, and Hans-Georg Gadamer. Michael arrived early, hoping to leaf through the newly published translation of Lyotard's *Lessons on the Analytic of the Sublime*. He found a table and ordered a pastis, a carafe of water, and some marinated olives. He observed his surroundings listlessly and began to think—something he always found to provide a satisfying degree of suffering.

Michael was contemplating the possibility of dedicating his spare time to the structural analysis of Dasein when he heard, from far away at first, then growing more and more insistent, the virile growl of a Harley Davidson, its vibrations causing the surroundings to resonate as if by symbiosis, dragging the other customers out of their reverent concentration one by one. Fear and anticipation loomed in the air, interlacing like a couple of teenagers embracing for the first time to the sound of rock 'n' roll. As the noise reached an almost unbearable crescendo— the vibrations under foot suggesting unusual seismic activity along the San Andreas Fault—the restaurant's side wall smashed open, revealing amid the rubble and severed and swaying electrical wires the glorious silhouette of Meat Loaf on his motorcycle, riding through a cloud of smoke and carbon monoxide toward Michael's table as the customers looked on in admiration.

After cocktails, roused by the rich vapors escaping the kitchen, the two men ordered something to eat. Michael went with the rosemary- and orange-crusted rack of lamb served with an exquisite ratatouille and baby pickled onions sprinkled with coarse sea salt, while Meat Loaf opted for the Mediterranean slow-braised osso buco with oven-roasted potatoes and ouzo-glazed carrots. As they quaffed a 1989 Beringer Third Century Syrah, they got past the pleasantries and down to business. Meat Loaf had always admired Michael's work and was eager for him to direct a music video for the first track off his new album, a Wagnerian rock anthem entitled "I'd Do Anything for Love (But I Won't Do That)." Bay knew the material well and welcomed the request. Firstly, the piece, which was eleven minutes and fifty-eight seconds long, would allow him to direct his longest work to date (the video would, however, in the end be based on the shorter version of the song, lasting seven minutes and thirty-eight seconds). Secondly, the theme of the work and its overall feel would enable him to pay cinematic homage to two works that marked his formative years, *The Phantom of the Opera* and *Beauty and the Beast*. Lastly, he would have the chance to ask the rock star about the meaning of the mysterious "that" punctuating his refrains, since a syntactic analysis, despite pointing to a few tentative conclusions, shed no definitive light on the word's ambiguity.

"So I've been wondering," said Michael, "what you're referring to when you say 'but I won't do that'...? Are you simply leaving it up to individual interpretation, or are you looking to cultivate a certain confusion with the same baroque logic that seems to define the piece?"

"I'd be lying if I said I wasn't expecting a question like that from you," Meat Loaf shot back with a mischievous smile. "The idea is definitely to create a certain level of confusion—nothing rubs me the wrong way like accessible art—but the real meaning of 'that' is far from abstract."

Michael looked at him, his mind a blank canvas.

"I usually avoid talking about it so directly when people ask me that question," continued Meat Loaf, "but I get the feeling your ability to grasp concepts far supersedes that of the average person. So here it is: the song is inspired by my relationship with Nell Campbell. We met on the set of *The Rocky Horror Picture Show* and clicked almost right away. We dated for a few months and shared everything; we'd often stay up till dawn discussing the meaning of love. For the first time, I felt complete. But then I started noticing subtle changes in her behavior. As if she were becoming more and more distant, or rather, as if she were holding something back that she wasn't ready to admit, to me at least. I asked her about it gently, letting her know that I realized something was different but that I wouldn't judge her, no matter what was on her mind. She finally told me, 'I no longer believe in the idea of systems. I think we should embrace the philosophical trend of anti-systems that's been around for the past half-century. Follow me on this path, Meat Loaf.' It was as if a stranger were standing in front of me. I would never abandon systems thinking. Embracing the opposite would be more than a sacrifice; it would make absolutely no sense. So we went our separate ways. Even for love, I'd never do that."

Enlightened, Michael asked, "So if the lyrics are that personal, why are they attributed to Jim Steinman?"

24

"Jim Steinman doesn't exist. I wanted to imbue the piece with an element of mystery, to move it away from the concrete so that it could come into its own in the absolute of art. Using my own name would have directly implicated Nell, which is in fact the truth but lacking any sort of magic. The pseudonym allowed me to be more detached, transforming my overall banal individual experience into something epic."

They shared a brief silence.

"I believe I can do your work justice," said Michael.

"And I, yours."

After that encounter, and following numerous other conversations with Meat Loaf, Michael was able to lay the groundwork for what would become his art. Thus began a fruitful collaboration between the two men; the music videos "Objects in the Rear View Mirror May Appear Closer Than They Are" and "Rock and Roll Dreams Come Through" would soon lead to Michael filming his first big explosions and developing a framework that he could use in the future.

But for the moment, Michael Bay and Meat Loaf finished their meal, attended the round table event and, being avid readers of Husserl, refuted Gadamer's arguments during the Q&A period.

ON THE IMPORTANCE OF BEING PUNCTUAL

SHIRT OPEN AND FLAPPING in the wind, the hot sun gleaming off his muscular sweat-covered torso, Michael Bay ran like mad through the crowded streets of Los Angeles, his fierce gaze filtering out everything between him and his goal. He made swift work of the numerous obstacles in his path: he jumped fences, skirted poles, soared over garbage cans and trash heaps, slid across car hoods, leapt up stairs three at a time, dodged stray bullets in sketchy neighborhoods, and narrowly avoided a few wheelchair basketball players (with apologies). He still had eight miles to cover in just twenty minutes if he wanted to arrive on time (and God knows he did) to what he believed might just be the most important meeting of his life. His destination: 10202 West Washington Boulevard, Culver City, headquarters of Sony Pictures Entertainment, where distinguished producers and brilliant minds Don Simpson and Jerry Bruckheimer awaited him at their Columbia office. Michael's excitement about the meeting—its exact nature still a mystery—was magnified by the fact that it was through Bruckheimer's gifted penmanship that he had, seventeen years earlier, first discovered Plato. The famous philosopher had quickly come to represent a father figure to the young boy, replacing the broken one whose late-discovered illegitimacy and dishonesty had negated any previous feelings of comfort. The first reading of all Plato's dialogues, though it had failed to offer up the immediate answers so desperately hoped for, helped Michael become an analytical thinker, the author's ideas, advice, and encouragements shaping his very soul. Plato's influence on Michael Bay thus went beyond the themes of his works. They encompassed the very notion of philosophy itself, which, more than the modern vision of the discipline as a space for reflecting on the mind itself, must espouse all the world's knowledge—from literature to geometry to metaphysics—to give rise to meaning. More than just a field of study, philosophy can be seen as the basis for everything, as a level (of thinking) that gives fundamental structure to the universe, accessible by a humanistic attitude toward knowledge. But the special father-son relationship Michael sought with his new role model presented a sizable problem: it lacked the warmth, affection, and physical connection that usually nourish heart and conscience. To fill the void, young Michael studied the philosopher's life with the hopes of making him more concrete. The fact that most Plato historians agree his biography (though widely accepted) was invented a posteriori to complement his works only added to Michael's emotional vertigo. Vertigo that became all the more real when Michael, still running at top speed, realized he was headed toward a fifty-foot drop. The "shortcut" he'd taken a few minutes earlier turned out to be a series of commercial-building rooftops that ended abruptly. Facing the inevitable and still determined to arrive on time at the Columbia Pictures lobby (which definitively ruled out turning back), he launched himself across the divide, praying the laws of physics would be on his side. Momentum propelled him a good distance from the ledge that marked the starting point of his leap into flight. In mid-air—his perception of time altered by potentially imminent death—Michael noted that the final point along the invisible curve being plotted by his body in motion would most likely be the roof of a taxi driving along the street below, if it maintained its current speed. His quick calculation proved correct. The sound of crumpling metal rang out as Michael landed spread-eagle on the car. As he grabbed hold of the taxi light to keep from falling off, the panicked driver, rather than brake and resolve the predicament in relative calmness, accelerated and started zigzagging along Venice Boulevard to dislodge the threat from the roof of his cab. Keeping a firm grip on the light, his legs buffeting from side to side, Michael fought to hold on a bit longer, as the taxi was in fact headed toward his final destination. A shot rang out and he felt a bullet whizz by inches from his right ear. He could now see into the backseat through a small hole in the roof. Projectiles continued to pierce the metal, grazing Michael's arms, legs, and sides, but never breaking the skin. The driver, increasingly frantic and unfocused, crashed headlong into a fire hydrant, sending the unwelcome passenger flying into the air. Just as Michael (whose years of training included basic gymnastics) absorbed the shock of the fall with an instinctive, graceful roll, a powerful jet of water from the city water main suddenly propelled the immobilized taxi into the air then dropped it onto its roof seconds later. Passersby stopped to observe the spectacular sight of the totaled vehicle, tempered by a rainbow springing up as the light hit millions of tiny droplets still shooting into the sky.

Michael walked through the production company doors with two minutes to spare. Just enough time to button his shirt, catch his breath, pop a mint in his mouth, and wipe his brow. The physical exertion had given him a healthy glow. After checking in with the receptionist—a tanned young man with dark, glistening hair, piercing blue eyes, and a perfectly toned body—Michael paced the lobby waiting to be called. A selection of artifacts from the studio's illustrious past were elegantly displayed between dozens of imposing white marble columns, including a suit worn by Clark Gable in *It Happened One Night* and a series of set photos from the acclaimed *Mr. Smith Goes to Washington* starring James Stewart, from an era when Columbia Pictures Corporation, after being the industry laughingstock for several years due to a series of dubious artistic decisions, had begun its ascent to new heights as one of Hollywood's "Little Three" (alongside Universal and United Artists). Next, a testament to the glorious forties, hung a dozen dresses once worn with panache by the legendary Rita Hayworth, alongside wax figures of The Three Stooges and a coat rack used for many years on the set of *Father Knows Best*, the studio's first television show. Then, a random assortment including the checkered jacket worn by Marlon Brando in *On The Waterfront*, a piece of the bridge on the River Kwai, Harold Ramis's coveralls (splattered with ectoplasm) from *Ghostbusters*, and the tree stump Ralph Macchio practiced his crane kicks on in *The Karate Kid*. A young man approached Michael, calling his name and cutting short his pleasant meanderings down memory lane.

"Hi, Michael, and welcome home!" he cried, to Michael's delight. "My name's Gregor, assistant to Mr. Simpson and Mr. Bruckheimer. If you could please follow me, they're ready for you."

Gregor was about the same age as Michael. His appearance was striking: he wore a t-shirt printed to look like the upper portion of a toga, complete with sculpted chest (Michael later learned it was the official shirt of the assistant's former fraternity), his arms were completely covered in tattoos, and he had black-and-white checkerboard Vans on.

"Are you into punk rock?" asked Michael as they walked.

"You could definitely say that. Ever heard of The Daredevils?"

"No... To be honest, I know the Ramones and Bad Religion and that's pretty much it."

"Oh... Well, you never know. It's my band. We're kind of under the radar still. But our lead singer is actually Brett Gurewitz. He's leaving Bad Religion to focus on The Daredevils. So that's really gonna help get our name out there. You should come to our next show!"

"Thanks... I'll do my best. I actually only know Bad Religion because I often run into Greg Gaffin at the bookstore near my house. He's a great guy. He's taught me a lot about anthropology and zoology."

"Right... Greg... Let's just say we're not on the best terms right now, what with everything going on with the band. So, you went to Wesleyan, right? I've always wanted to meet Basinger—she's such a big name! Did you like it there?"

The two men discussed their film studies education for a few minutes longer as they continued on to meet Simpson and Bruckheimer. Gregor was a graduate of the state's prestigious UCLA Film School. He'd also done a stint in commercial directing, though with less success than the man he was escorting toward a certain future.

His heart beating notably faster, Michael followed Gregor into the office where the producers who had called him in usually spent their days. The space was massive and awe-inspiring: it too was bordered by a series of imposing white columns, and the central room, covered with a plush carpet, was surrounded by smaller rooms accessible through porticos joining the

31

colonnades. The main room, illuminated by enormous skylights, seemed empty (aside from the strong smell of sweat and chalk powder that hung in the air), while the surrounding rooms appeared to each have specific functions. There was a cloakroom, dining room, projection room, library, sauna, small workout room (with stationary bikes, free weights, and training machines), massage room, classroom, sitting room for casual discussion, observatory with skylights, shower, and storage area. After taking off his shoes and following Gregor to the sitting room, Michael received a warm, enthusiastic greeting from Bruckheimer, who thanked Gregor with an affectionate—and slightly sensual—ruffle of his hair. Once Gregor had left in the direction of the workout room, Michael took a seat on one of the many leather sofas. Jerry Bruckheimer did the same. It was then that the young man noticed Don Simpson, even more intimidating and staggeringly aloof than he could have imagined. He was seated in a wingback armchair, sipping a bitter *sketo* and eyeing him with a calm, piercing gaze. Noting his guest's discomfort (Michael was smiling politely, lips pursed, staring at the wall), the friendlier of the two producers broke the ice.

"Tell us, Michael, how familiar are you with the literature on decolonization?"

"Decolonization? Somewhat. I read Aimé Césaire's *Notebook of a Return to the Native Land* when I was quite young."

"Oh! Césaire! Very good. And did you like it?"

"Yes, very much! I have to admit that I was only ten when I read the poem for the first time.

"Some of the passages went over my head, both in terms of language and subject, but I was fascinated by the text nonetheless. It moved me in ways I still can't quite pinpoint, if that makes sense. I felt that by rereading it again and again, I'd eventually be able to fully grasp it in all its complexity. At that age I suppose I liked the text's potential more than the text itself—something I often find, I'll admit. I added the book to the stack on my bedside table and would go back to it often, enjoying it more with every reading. To be honest though, I haven't opened it in a while. There's simply too much to read. I can still remember a few lines, though. Can't get them out of my head! *A man screaming is not a dancing bear...*"

"*But who misleads my voice? Who grates my voice? Stuffing my throat with a thousand bamboo fangs. A thousand sea urchin stakes. It is you dirty end of the world. Dirty end of the wee hours. It is you dirty hatred. It is you weight of the insult and a hundred years of whip lashes. It is you one hundred years of my patience, one hundred years of my effort simply to stay alive.*"

"*Yes!! So much blood in my memory! In my memory are lagoons. They are covered with death's-heads. They are not covered with water lilies. In my memory are lagoons. No women's loincloths spread out on their shores. My memory is encircled with blood. My memory has a belt of corpses!*"

"for it is not true that the work of man is done / that we have no business being on earth / that we parasite the world / that it is enough for us to heel to the world / whereas the work has only begun / and man still must overcome all the interdictions wedged in the recesses of his fervor."

"Put up with me. I won't put up with you!"

"I expected nothing less from you, Michael."

A moment passed. Everyone smiled.

"And in terms of theory?" continued Bruckheimer.

"I've done some reading, but I don't claim to be an expert on the subject."

"Some reading?"

"Well, my love of Césaire led me to his speech "What is Négritude to Me" and his *Discourse on Colonialism*, both very enlightening, but too brief for my taste. I've also read Albert Memmi's two Portraits, which I found highly stimulating and clearly articulated. If I remember correctly, I particularly enjoyed his reflection on the concept of the colonizer as usurper. And, of course, the symbiotic dynamic that unites opposing forces in a colonial setting. I know a little about Fanon too, but only from conversations on alienation I've had with friends."

"All French-speaking writers then. Do you speak French?"

"Some. I took classes for two semesters in college, but I don't have anyone to practice with, so I'm losing it a bit... But I come across French texts from time to time, and I can still understand them for the most part."

"And post-colonialism. How does that figure in?"

"Post-colonial theory didn't move me as much. Maybe because it's less visceral. Or because it wasn't born out of suffering."

Bruckheimer stared silently at Michael for a few seconds, his head shifting in an almost imperceptible vertical oscillation that was either approval or a simple acknowledgment. Whatever the case, a conclusion was clearly being formed, which caused further fraying to Michael's already taut nerves. Bruckheimer turned to Simpson and the two producers exchanged an unbearably neutral and equally indecipherable look, as though they were communicating via absolute telepathy. Feeling completely vulnerable, like a soldier awaiting a court martial verdict, Michael began to look distractedly around in an effort to soothe his nerves: on the walls hung portraits of great minds, one after the other (he recognized Kant, Heidegger, Foucault, Spinoza, and Montesquieu), as well as elegantly framed pictures from the set of *Top Gun*, whose theme song immediately began playing in his head—another calming strategy. Lost in Harold Faltermeyer's glorious electric guitar riffs, Michael reflected in fascination on the room's confusingly cohesive décor. Then Bruckheimer shook him from his reverie.

"The fact is, Don and I have been toying for some time now with the idea of doing a film that brings decolonization to a wider audience. We've already gotten several actors on board. We want you to direct it."

Two months later, cameras were rolling on the set of *Bad Boys*.

ON THE ENTHUSIASM OF ONE PROFESSOR

A HOARSE, acrid cough stirs Michael from his boozy slumber. Another dreamless night. His mouth, throat, and nostrils are dry as the Mojave Desert in June. The back of the chaise lounge where he's spent the last few hours is adjusted wrong, one side higher than the other, which explains the back pain that hits him when he tries to sit up for a minute. His head ticks like a bomb about to go off. Momentarily blinded by the sun's reflection in the pool, he sits with his satin robe wide open, his Optimus Prime boxers stained with blood and Blue Curaçao.

The backyard of Michael's Malibu mansion looks every bit like one of the sets where, for the last few years, he's been directing the destruction of objects and certainties. Fifty or so guests are strewn about like corpses, half-asleep or unconscious, some naked, some in costumes, others covered in permanent marker. Cuba Gooding Jr. floats by motionless on an inflatable mattress, an arrow and the words "insert knowledge here" scrawled across his ass. Glass shards, empty and half-empty bottles, confetti, food, and vomit cover the lawn. Festive splotches of multicolored paint can be seen here and there, mainly concentrated on an enormous canvas where the guests had gotten creative with paint-ball guns. A huge crystal bowl rests on a plastic patio table, finger marks disturbing an otherwise perfectly smooth coating of whitish powder. At the edge of the grounds, a felled tree leans against the dented roof of a shed next to a severed, quivering power line spewing sparks into a hot tub full of murky water. A baby sits on an American flag beach towel, squealing with delight as it plays with a silicone implant. The shell of a special edition Camaro lies smoldering on a stretch of pavement near the house—a sad memento of an enormous bonfire. The remnants of the premiere after-party suggest the evening was a success.

On his way to the house, Michael pretends not to hear the few groans—cries for help or hydration—float-ing up from a mass of bodies that give his property the look of a battlefield. Every step between him and the ibuprofen resonates in his skull. As he comes in through the veranda, a strong smell of sex floating in the living room brings on a wave of nausea. The carnage is extensive, rivaling the work of a professional demo-lition team. The massacred furniture, walls, floors, and ceilings have a strangely calming effect on Michael, as though an interior decorator had managed to distill his soul. A disciplined artist, he holds off on replenishing his electrolytes for a moment, grabs his notebook and a piece of charcoal, and does a rough sketch of the ransacked abode. These drawings will no doubt be useful for storyboarding *Bad Boys 2*, recently commissioned by the studio.

The second floor remains for the most part untouched by the partiers. In the comfort of his office, Michael chases a few tablets down with a kale smoothie. He sits down at his computer and taps the side of the mouse with his index finger to wake the monitor up. Where to begin? *The New York Times*? *The Hollywood Reporter*? *The Washington Post*? The room seems to be spinning ever so slightly. He closes his eyes, focuses on his breathing, fights the nausea. He places a wastepaper basket within reach. "This is it," he tells himself. "This time they'll get it."

On *The New York Times* website, the top story is an explosion at a Chicago chocolate factory. Michael scrolls to the Arts section, but can't find anything on his film. He sits stock-still, trying to breathe. Continuing to the Entertainment section, his mouth fills with bile as he reads the headline: "Pearl Harbor: A Good Reason to Stay In." Two out of five stars. According to the *Post*, his latest film is nothing more than a "failed, heavy-handed attempt at trying to recreate James Cameron's *Titanic*." Two and a half stars out of five. *Slate* calls it "ridiculously long, incoherent, and sometimes downright embarrassing." One and a half stars. Michael swivels in his chair and bends over the wastepaper basket, painful stomach spasms producing nothing but a few thick gobs of saliva that cling to his lips. Beads of sweat form at his temples. He decides to check a few discussion-forum reviews to see what the real filmgoers have to say. Michael focuses only on those written with at least some semblance of eloquence, skimming over several gushing reviews whose questionable grammar suggests a lack of real insight. The words *confusing, immature,* and *macho* stand out; as do comparisons of him to the antichrist, and the newly coined terms *bayhem* and *baydiocre.* No mention of the film's critique of US military arrogance, the underlying parody behind its approach mid-way between satire and homage to the epic historical sub-genre, or the examination of ethical constraints imposed by the fictionalization of real characters. Once again, nobody gets it.

Michael leans back in his desk chair and stares at the ceiling, breathing through his mouth, feeling awful. The truth doesn't sit well. He straightens up, opens a small cigar box, takes out a generous pinch of marijuana, and stuffs it into his calabash pipe. He inhales a few puffs, which brings some relief, closely followed by feelings of guilt, cowardice, and shame. His high is a tightrope stretched across the void, the air around him like cotton wool soaked in peroxide. The ping of his inbox pulls him from his stupor.

The preliminary box office results are coming in and seems like the promo did the trick: it's looking like the most lucrative opening weekend of your career! Michael, Michael, Michael... You were already rich, but now even those Saudi princes will be green with envy. Take a few days off. You deserve it!

I'm meeting Jerry next week at the office to talk about where we go from here.

It's such a pleasure working with you. You're a true genius!
Sophy Stanislas
Line Producer
Touchstone Pictures

Michael stares for a few seconds at the last sentence and, in an uncharacteristic fit of rage, grabs the screen with both hands, jumps up, and throws it out the window and into the pool. He tries to take deep breaths to calm himself down, but can't stop trembling. He looks at the pipe, thinks "no," then picks it up and takes a few more hits anyway. He sinks back down into his chair and stares at the wall for a while. Someone is ringing the doorbell. Dazed, Michael brings his hands to his face and kneads his eyelids with his knuckles. He coughs, takes a sip of smoothie, and opens a desk drawer. On top of a pile of papers sits a framed photo of Michael and Danny, his college roommate, smiling with their arms around each other. On the back, the words "Wesleyan - 1985" are written on a piece of masking tape. Michael sighs and places the picture on the desk

where his monitor used to be. What he is really looking for is a somewhat battered document whose cover
page reads: ON POETRY AND ITS RELATIONSHIP
TO TIME IN THE MOVIE *STALKER*. By Michael Bay.
Presented to Ms. Jeanine Basinger. FILM2334, National
Cinemas: Eastern Europe. December 15, 1983. Wesleyan
University. Michael leafs through it until he gets to the
very last page and re-reads the words in red pen for
the umpteenth time: "Highly impressive and unusually
insightful. The writing is elegant, lively, and a pleasure
to read. You're a bright mind with a bright future. A+."

He hugs the paper to his chest and, ignoring the
doorbell still ringing downstairs, bursts into tears.

ON WORKING WITH ACTORS

WILL SMITH sat curled up on the couch crying, face contorted and head in his hands. His trailer—the inside at least—was a mess. Open, dog-eared books lay strewn across the floor among shards of broken glass. A hole in the wall slightly bigger than a clenched fist offered a view inside the small bathroom, where a makeup table, now devoid of its contents, leaned on its side against a wall. Blackish smoke rose from a smattering of embers in the sink, and the walls, stripped of their posters, were now bare except for a few leftover corners held in place by bits of tape. Just as Smith grabbed a pack of cigarettes near the sofa only to find it empty, heightening his already visible distress, Martin Lawrence walked up in a black tank top and baggy burgundy vest, and knocked on the door.

"Get lost!" snapped Smith, a little choked up. "Leave me alone!"

"Will, it's Martin. I just want to talk. Everything's cool, Will. I just want to chat, OK? Can I come in? I brought that salami you like."

Lawrence took the silence as a yes, opened the door with a charming smile, and entered the scene of a still-fresh, full-blown tantrum.

"Taking deconstruction literally, I see."

"Another comment like that is going to land you a black eye."

A smiling Lawrence placed the pick-me-up gift on a side table that was still upright. The elegant two-inch-thick cherrywood board held a carefully and tastefully chosen selection of three kinds of ham, roast pork, roast beef, Hungarian salami, Syrah and five-pepper sausage, various terrines (wild boar, venison, and pheasant), rillettes (duck and rabbit), and pâtés (goose and truffle, foie gras), as well as an assortment of mustards (old-fashioned Reims, Burgundy white wine, and a grape-juice, sundried tomato and Espelette hot pepper blend), pork aspic, a fresh baguette, and pickled vegetables (mainly gherkins but also carrots, mushrooms, and cauliflower). Despite having eaten just two hours earlier, the two actors dug in, more out of a love of food than actual hunger. After a few minutes of silence, broken only by a few brief remarks of consensus about the quality of the flavors, Lawrence made the first move, as always.

"So, you're pissed at Michael?"

"The thing is, he makes me feel like an idiot. I'm sure he knows what he's doing, but shit, it's like I'll never be good enough. Like I can never give him the performance he's looking for, even though I know I can get there. And

43

I really hate the goddamn feeling that I can't measure up."

"Will, it's not that bad. Honestly, I think he's happy with what you're doing. You're Will Smith! The Fresh Prince of Bel-Air! The most charismatic guy I know!"

"Charisma is one thing; talent and depth are something else."

"Don't give me that 'depth' shit. Everybody knows you're no idiot. Or if you are, you're the first idiot I've met who can spout Artaud, *Tao Te King*, and Bourdieu in the same clear, convincing sentence."

"Just because I can cite a few texts I've read doesn't mean I understand them perfectly. In fact I always feel like I know nothing! There's a difference between knowing how to reference ideas and really *talking* about them. I'm always so superficial, and it makes me sick. Shit... And now I'm spending every day with Michael Bay, a goddamn *wunderkind* who's inspiring, sure, but who pisses me off because he's too good."

"Listen, Will. Nobody has all the answers, Michael included. He's not as confident as he seems, you know. It's just that he's always questioning things, voicing his doubts. He makes mistakes like everybody else. But he's a hard worker and a bright guy, just like you. Listen, I think it'd be good for you two to talk. He always has good advice."

Smith sighed.

"Yeah, I guess you're right. I'll go see him later."

"You know—and this is just a suggestion—maybe he could join us for this feast, like, right now?"

Smith gave Lawrence a look. He realized he'd been outplayed but wasn't bitter. With an exaggerated smile, Lawrence knocked three times on the inside of the trailer door. Michael came straight in, a few bottles of Brouilly and San Pellegrino in hand.

"I don't know about you, but all this delicious meat is making me thirsty!" said Lawrence, pleased with himself.

"Will," said Michael as he filled their glasses. "Seriously, that last take was great. You were funny, in-your-face, concentrated, articulate—it was really good! You're *this* close to that perfect, memorable performance... you're just missing a touch of sensitivity."

"I know, I know... It's just hard to figure out exactly what kind of 'sensitive' you're looking for. It's not like I can start crying in the middle of a scene like that, you know? Especially since I personally feel like the scene's not that important, kind of insignificant."

"Ah, but that's where you're wrong, Will," continued Michael. "I see this scene as being at the very heart of what we're trying to do with the film. It's the kind of scene where your sensitivity is going to give a whole new historical depth to our approach. Listen—you too, Martin—the goal of this scene is for you to really become the Bad Boys. Let's put things in perspective: first of all, you're both black men. You're victims of systematic racism, you're considered amoral and ontologically inferior to whites. From there, the film's premise flips things around. You're two black *police officers*.

You represent authority, the law, the good guys. You're in control: Miami is your city. That's the starting point."

"So..." Lawrence interrupted. "The opening scene, the one with the carjacking, that's pretty much to get all that across. To show that we're on our turf, and we're in control. Our Miami is precolonial Africa."

"Exactly!" answered Bay, biting into a pickle. "Except then things get more complicated: that order is broken through usurpation. The criminals (who are all white), led by a French guy (also white), break into the station and steal the literal fruits of your labor—in this case the drugs you've just confiscated. After that, they hold the power. Driven by a thirst for justice, you want to take back what's yours, but the oppressor, who wants nothing more than to knock you down, seems completely out of reach. So you start to doubt yourselves, which creates tension. It's that tension we see in this afternoon's scene, when Will's character starts to feel like people don't fully appreciate him for what he's worth. And Martin's character, alienated by jealousy, goes so far as to become an advocate for the oppressor by judging you based on your lineage, which you find totally unfair and disgusting. So, when I was talking about sensitivity, what I meant was when you say your lines about your inheritance and all the hard work you put in, I want you to keep in mind that you're also expressing all the rage of your ancestors: their humiliation at a time when they were refused any kind of dignity or human respect."

Smith nodded, beginning to understand.

"It's important to get this scene right because it's a truly pivotal moment in the film. After that rebellion, which follows a brief moment where Martin seems to want to give up the fight, you have an epiphany: you both realize that the only way to overcome adversity and regain control is to reclaim what is, within this antagonist discourse, attributed to you by default, that is, the 'Bad Boys' label given to your race. By reclaiming this label, you turn the situation around and are once again in a position of power. That scene in the car is the emergence of *Négritude*. You wear the trophy of "repugnant ugliness" and draw from it a new subversive force that will allow you to win the fight in the end. And then the strategic use of cliché is emphasized by the urge your characters suddenly feel to start rapping—a clear reference to the stereotype of the black man who's got rhythm. Get it?"

"Got it," replied Smith.

"Got it," replied Lawrence.

"Make sense?" continued Michael.

"Makes sense."

"Makes sense."

And so the team waited for the light to echo the soft amber of daybreak and the scene was filmed with such precision and emotion that Will Smith, moved by the power of his words, broke down in tears as Michael called, "Cut."

ON ATTRACTION

MICHAEL DRIFTED FROM ONE SHELF to the next, deep in the throes of never-ending literary research. He had always felt safe in the calmness of bookstores, often lingering long after he had found the book he had come in for—in this case, a copy of *La dépossession du monde* by Jacques Berque, which numerous bibliographies and footnotes had led him to. He had quickly found the volume, but, drawn in by the vast array of titles and their equally numerous possibilities, he then wandered slowly and aimlessly about, dreamily browsing, stopping to read a blurb here and there without making it to the end of any, constantly distracted. He was overwhelmed by the sheer quantity, his burning desire to read every book preventing him from getting through a single sentence. But it was a satisfying feeling, like an enlightened form of mental relaxation.

He was staring blankly at the back of a Bret Easton Ellis novel, rereading the same five words over and over, reflecting on them in no particular order, when a voice roused him from his reverie.

"Michael? Michael Bay?"

Michael looked up and turned to see who it was. He had spent his life around beautiful women: the satisfied clients of his adoptive father who were regularly invited to use the pool at their modern and impressively large white house; models and other well-endowed nymphets who had on numerous occasions paraded in front of his lenses; and average California girls. Michael had been surrounded by bimbos to such an extent that, while he still had an appreciation for the charms of a svelte silhouette, female beauty no longer unsettled him as it used to. But the young woman who was speaking to him sent him into a state of complete vulnerability. The fact that he couldn't manage to place her, even though she clearly knew his name, was in itself unsettling; however, the mental paralysis that seized him was more the result of pure attraction. The stranger was pretty despite not being a stereotypical buxom blond: she had straight, dark, shoulder-length brown hair, thick-framed glasses, fair skin, fine features, and an unassuming smile.

"You don't recognize me, do you? It's Daphné."

Her deep brown eyes, the epicenter of her charm, oozed intelligence. Slightly narrowed in a mirthful, yet constantly analytic way, they couldn't be further from the distracted gaze that characterized most Los Angeles women, giving the almost intimidating impression that she was always *there*, well-rooted in the moment, ready to react to any eventuality with tact, spirit, and good judgment.

49

"Daphné Couture, from the Metz seminar... At Wesleyan!"

While clearly aware of her natural endowments, she did not make a show of them, possessed by a calculated sense of modesty that lent her an aura of mysterious grace. Transfixed by her gaze, Michael Bay was struck by the poetic beauty of her intellect, which was far more bewitching than any plastic perfection. She looked at him, enthusiastically, kindly, waiting for him to reply.

"The talk on Antonioni?... I hosted a party after the last session at my place."

She spoke with an accent from the North that evoked rivers and wide-open spaces. Michael realized that he hadn't budged for about twenty seconds, gathered his thoughts, and collected himself.

"Yes, Daphné! I'm sorry, Daphné. Of course I remember you. You asked me a very interesting question after my lecture on *RoboCop 2*. We kind of butted heads and everyone else thought we were being too intense, it was funny. Then we talked about Antonioni again and made up. And later at the party at your place, you forgot to wear oven mitts when you took out the cookies, and you burned yourself. You've changed a bit, that's the only reason I hesitated."

Daphné seemed reassured.

"I'm glad to hear that's what people remember about me," she said teasingly. "Well *I* definitely won't forget—I still have a nice scar on both hands. At least the cookies were good!"

Michael smiled, charmed by her knack for self-deprecation and irony.

"You live in LA, now?"

"Yes, I have for a few months. I ended up leaving Connecticut. I was there to do my PhD at Wesleyan, but I didn't really get along with my advisor. Anyway, I got fed up so I left, and now I'm finishing it at UCLA. I'm really liking it. My new advisor is a lot better, even though I had to change my thesis topic a bit. Anyway..."

"A PhD... that's great! The world needs people like you. What's your thesis on?"

"I'm looking at the representation of the mother as a cathartic mechanism for the sublime in the work of Visconti and Proust. The topic itself is really interesting, but my day-to-day is actually pretty boring. And you? It seems like things are going pretty well. You're doing tons of ads and clips—that's so cool! I always figured you'd be successful."

"Thanks, that's nice of you. I'm not complaining, that's for sure, especially since I'm working on my first feature film right now with Bruckheimer and Simpson—a big Columbia production. I've finally gotten the chance, I think, to do a project that lives up to my ambitions. It's on decolonization. Hence this book by Berque. It's exciting stuff!"

Daphné looked at Michael, as though unconsciously satisfied by their encounter, as though something had clicked between them. Admittedly, she found him sexy:

51

his slightly unruly chestnut hair; his gentle, determined blue eyes; his athletic build, all of which added to his obvious intellectual sensibility. Though her academic ambitions required regular participation in these kinds of conversations, as a rule she wasn't comfortable with drawn-out banalities. She always managed to find some place she "really had to be" after the required and somewhat self-promotional exchange of pleasantries. Not that she couldn't hold a conversation—she could—but no matter how her intelligence shone, she secretly feared the judgment and differing opinions of others. But this time, Daphné didn't feel the need for an exit strategy. She felt warm, safe, at home.

"Do you have plans tonight?" she ventured.

"I'm actually due at the airport in forty-five minutes. We're heading back to Miami to shoot on location. I'll be there for the next three weeks."

"Oh... OK, well good luck. Maybe we'll run into each other again once you're back."

They shared a brief silence. Gazes locked, they looked deep into each other's eyes.

"If you don't have plans, maybe you could come to Miami. We're taking the company plane and there's plenty of room. And there's a huge budget for this film, so all expenses would be covered. You could come back to LA whenever you want. What do you think?"

"Alright, sure! It'd be nice to have a break," Daphné blurted out, to her surprise. "I just need to stop by my place and grab some clothes and a few other things..."

"There's not really time. You can buy new clothes in Miami. I should be able to scrounge up five or ten thousand in the budget."

Ordinarily a rational long-term thinker, Daphné happily gave in to impulse. Without further delay, they hopped onto Michael's gleaming motorcycle and headed into the sunset toward the Santa Monica airport. As they approached the runway, five fighter jets roared overhead, slicing a glorious V into the blue of the sky. Michael, compelled by the artistic potential of the moment, raised his fist in a dramatic salute.

SCREAMING AND TEARING at their faces, a group of women knelt before the coffin. Inside, locks of hair had been scattered across the corpse as some sort of tribute.

The room was bathed in golden light. Perched atop a Hollywood hill, the funeral parlor was decorated with statues and colonnades, giving it an air of classical beauty. Hundreds of people had gathered there on that January afternoon, some truly shattered by the death, others attracted by the glamour of such a funeral. The trendiest caterer in town had been hired. The hottest DJ reigned over the room, perched behind his turntable, adding his personal flair to the ceremonial silence. The tuxedos—like the wailing women's faces—were all clearly designer made.

Eyes swollen and jaw clenched, Michael stared blankly from a corner of the room, a stuffed vine leaf in his hand, still untouched. Around him, he saw few familiar faces. He didn't quite know if he should be paying respects or receiving them. A man in his fifties with a waxed moustache and numerous rings on his fingers walked over to him.

"Are you family?"

"It's complicated."

The man kept talking, but Michael wasn't listening, lost in his own thoughts. Who were all these people? How could this have happened? Could he have done things differently? Was there something he was supposed to learn from all this? Was it possible to ever really understand anything? The crowd blurred together into a sea of faces, some more bereft than others, yet all evenly tanned. But one person stood out. On the other side of the room, half hidden by the crowd, a man who looked vaguely Mediterranean was staring straight at him. Michael tried to lock his gaze, to force his eyebrows into a look of confrontation, but the man didn't react. Maybe he was actually staring at the gentleman next to Michael, who hadn't stopped talking. "Such a tragedy. So young... And the circumstances... So sad..."

"I... Yes, it's tragic, truly tragic."

Michael hadn't eaten in three days. His brain could no longer keep up with his racing mind. The man's incessant chatter was eroding his already precarious concentration. In a fraction of a second, he had lost sight of the man with the menacing look, who had vanished like a well-trained Marine. No doubt an hors d'oeuvre or two would have helped the situation, but that was impossible given his knotted stomach. Michael closed his eyes as tightly as he could, shook his head as though to reboot his cognitive functions, then stretched out his neck to make a half-hearted sweep of the room.

"Are you alright? Is it the grief? Are you still listening?"

"Sorry? I... Uh... Excuse me."

Michael entrusted the still-oily grape leaf to the mustachioed man's care and made his way into the sea of people. "You're just as boring as your movies..." he could hear from behind. Gritting his teeth, but unusually unwilling to debate the point, he kept going. The crowd was thick. A dozen American flags hung from the ceiling. Michael had reached the middle of the room but, despite carefully scanning the crowd, still couldn't spot the man he was beginning to suspect he might have imagined. It suddenly hit him that, other than the group of crying women, all of the guests were men. No doubt the women were in some antechamber, observing customs he was, regrettably, unfamiliar with. He also noticed that the coffin had not been placed along the wall, but rather with the body's feet pointing toward the entrance of the room. Suddenly, behind an enormous floral arrangement decorating the casket, the furtive, olive-skinned face reappeared, still staring at Michael. What could he want? Determined to confront the man, Michael attempted to move toward him when his path was suddenly blocked by a giant of a man with a grip mid-way between camaraderie and intimidation. The brute seemed vaguely familiar: Michael thought perhaps he had seen him at the *Bad Boys* premiere talking with Don Simpson. He reeked of money and faulty logic.

"Cheer up, Michael. Now you can finally stand on your own two feet! Isn't that wonderful? You should see this death as liberating, like a springboard, not an obstacle. Everything happens for a reason, you know."

For a moment, Michael completely forgot about the man he was following.

"How dare you? The person you're talking about made me who I am today, opened me up to a whole new world. And you want me to be happy? Who do you think you are, talking to me like that?"

"Michael, Michael... Save it for the eulogy. We're all friends here. I'm well aware the relationship meant a lot to you, but hasn't it brought you more suffering than happiness lately? Hasn't it left you plagued by doubt?"

"I've always doubted. Doubt is a good thing."

"If you say so. You're looking good, though. Really happy. Thriving, even."

Michael paused for a moment. Behind the bouquets, there was no trace of the Mediterranean man.

"I'll ask you again: who do you think you are?"

"And I'll tell you again: I'm a friend. You know there are few things I care about more than your career. You have enormous potential. You know, Michael, I've already invested a lot in your success. You should be thanking me. Did you not appreciate the tête-à-têtes with those screenwriters I sent over to put a bit of order into your recent shoot? They're very good, aren't they?

Don't get me wrong: so are you! It's just that you sometimes lose your way a bit. There's no shame in accepting help."

"You call that help? It's sabotage, that's what it is! Your two buffoons completely ruined my film."

"Don't forget that you work for the public and that the public has certain expectations. Just take a look at the market studies. It's the public that pays for your luxury cars. Not posterity. Not bookworms. Don't be naive. You seem like you've got brains; you need to use them."

Michael was outraged by the man's lecture, but a new sighting of the Mediterranean eclipsed his desire to respond. This time, he felt certain that the man spying on him was not, in fact, a figment of his exhausted imagination. He'd felt for months that someone was watching him. When his observer, half hidden behind the buffet table, pulled out a camera and pointed it at him, he felt something click inside him. It was the same feeling he'd had when he had lost his cool a few weeks earlier on the streets of San Francisco. He tensed, shoved past the charismatic executive and quickened his pace in the direction of the stranger, who remained imperturbable. "Paparazzi," he muttered, "another paparazzi son-of-a-bitch. This time, you're mine. You don't have your Hummer to save you now." The air had an orange glow. The atmosphere was solemn; whispers could be heard beneath the keening of the women. Michael's briskness was at odds with the decorum of the scene. Predator turned prey, the photographer realized he had to leave, and fast, or, judging by Michael's eyes, his future would be grim. Holed up behind the canapés, tartares, and olives, he could not, however, spot an easy exit since the guests were gathered around the food, blocking his way. Michael picked up his pace and pushed through more of the guests, stirring up a commotion. The photographer was, like an enemy MiG, locked in his sights. Sixty feet from his target, Michael leaped and slid across the buffet table as if it were a car hood, grabbing the man by the neck and pinning him to the wall.

"It's your fault she's gone! You paparazzi scumbags! You destroy lives with your cameras! Don't you understand? Daphné never wanted anything to do with you! You've ruined everything! Everything!"

The photographer's oniony breath and greasy hair were repellent. Nevertheless, Michael shouted mere inches from his face, "Stop following me, you parasites! Vultures! You want me to tell you what meaning is? Well I don't know! But I know one thing: your life doesn't have any! Stop sucking the life out of other people! You rats! Who do you work for? What's going on at the Apollo gym? What do the orange trees mean? Why are you following me?"

Bruckheimer intervened, stepping between the two men. The photographer coughed loudly, clutching his throat. Michael realized that an uneasy silence had fallen over the room, and everyone was staring at him in surprise. "You—get out of here!" said Bruckheimer to the Mediterranean, which he did, while the rest of the room remained perfectly still. The air felt heavy. Bruckheimer shot a look at Michael, who got the message and shamefacedly apologized to the crowd. The women resumed their weeping.

The producer and his protégé moved their conversation to the next room.

"Michael, you have to control yourself. Making a scene like that, here of all places... What were you thinking?"

"I... I don't know... I'm so tired."

"I realize that this is a sad ordeal, but try to keep a cool head. Hang onto your dignity. Never let your heart control your mind. Your intellect is much too precious. You still have a lot to learn, Michael."

"All of this is so absurd. How can we begin to comprehend the incomprehensible? How can we make sense of something when meaning itself is such an elusive concept?"

"I'm not here to give you answers, son. I'm here to spark questions."

"I don't know that I can handle any more questions. Everything around me is so uncertain, so unclear. It's exhausting. Doubt has always been the cornerstone of my life, but I don't know that I'm strong enough to withstand another shock. The only thing that seems tangible to me right now is my thirst for revenge."

"Revenge is part of the language of the heart. An intelligent man always works to dispel his hate through analysis and nuance."

"What's the point of analysis and nuance if they just lead to inaction? I'm not a spectator. I'm a creator. I take action! I swear, I'm going to find whoever was responsible and I'm going to..."

A slap brought his speech to an abrupt halt. Michael raised his hand to his cheek, challenged Bruckheimer with a wild look, then quickly thought better of it out of respect for his mentor.

"Don't be stupid, Michael. There are things we have absolutely no control over. Perhaps your role as a director has given you the illusion that you're in control, but life is not a movie set. Try to focus on the positive. *The Rock* has just come out. Crowds are flocking to see it. You're getting your message across."

"My message? *My* message? You mean the studio's message!"

"You'll have to be satisfied with that for now. A message disguised is still better than no message at all."

There was a brief silence.

"You're probably right. I'm not thinking straight."

"You should rest. Eat something. We have a big day tomorrow."

The sun was now low on the horizon. Michael stepped back into the main hall and was reassured by the crowd's seeming indifference: the small scandal he'd caused was already old news. His gaze lowered, he walked over to the buffet, took a few deep breaths, and managed to swallow a few squid tentacles, his digestive juices more than happy to get to work. His heart still heavy with loss, he stopped to pay his last respects to the corpse, made a short stop at the washroom to slip into something more comfortable, then left the funeral parlor for Orange County behind the wheel of his pick-up, an impressive supply of explosives stashed in the back.

ON PARENTAL FIGURES

AT THE AGE OF TWO, Michael Bay was adopted by Harriett Stamper, a professor of literature at the University of California, Los Angeles (UCLA) specializing in American and French poetry (her doctoral thesis, defended in 1964, was titled "Transatlantic Filiations: From Whitman to Ginsberg and Aragon"), and Jim Bay, a plastic surgeon in the midst of forging a reputation as a "magician" and "career-booster" among women with acting or modeling ambitions. Though they were not his blood relations—a detail kept from him for the first eleven years of his life, providing an illusion of legitimacy which proved, overall, beneficial to his early development—Harriett and Jim raised Michael in the comfort and relative tranquility of the Californian upper-middle class, which, for quite some time, guaranteed a certain familial stability many would be thankful for. In a modern and impressively large white house that was the envy of many in their new San Fernando Valley neighborhood, the happy young Bay family always

managed, despite Harriett and Jim's hectic and sometimes unpredictable schedules, to brighten their daily
lives with activities that allowed them to enjoy life's
simple pleasures while reinforcing the familial bond:
roadside picnics along the way to their weekend home
in Orange County; afternoons in San Francisco spent
riding cable cars, admiring the Golden Gate Bridge, or
visiting the mysterious island of Alcatraz; and monthly
hang gliding excursions over the Burbank Studios and
the Los Angeles Basin—an enormous body of water that
gave Michael his first taste of freedom and grandeur.
Quite frankly the Bays heaped attention and love on the
boy, so much so that they began, little by little, to forget
he was adopted.

Michael developed into a calm yet enthusiastic child
with a sense of curiosity that his parents continuously
fed. From his father, he learned discipline, herpetology,
rudimentary chemistry, high standards (for himself
and others), baseball, basic mechanics, woodworking,
and how to use recreational firearms. His father also
nurtured a fervent passion for car racing of all kinds
(from Formula 1, NASCAR, IndyCar, and stock cars,
to karting, a sport that allowed them to track the new
generation of promising drivers—the stars of tomorrow). From his mother, he learned to cultivate a taste
for the arts (literature, of course, but also the visual arts,
music, architecture, dance, theater, and film), as well as
for history, beauty, abstraction, systematization, debate,
research (and discovery), cheese, and political science,

not to mention a sense of altruism and an openness to other cultures.

While young Michael did not master all this knowledge straightaway, a basic understanding of each of these concepts set him apart in the classroom, which soon became one of his—if not his most—favorite of places. Michael was labeled a gifted student early on, which did not, however, hinder his ability to maintain healthy, rewarding interpersonal relationships. His numerous questions, though innocently posed, embarrassed his teachers on more than one occasion, reminded as they were of their own mediocrity. Elementary school was a place of comfort and growth for Michael Bay, his thirst for knowledge as yet unimpeded by the need to specialize. This need would be the start of his soul searching, planting the seed of doubt and triggering in him an acute pain at being unable, at least at the institutional level, to grow as a humanist.

"I ALREADY TOLD YOU: there is no Michael here. Now, please stop bothering me. I have a term paper to finish. Otherwise I'm going to have to call campus security. Do you really want harassment charges filed against you?"

The young man closed the door firmly, looked through the peephole to make sure the couple had indeed left, then went back to his desk where a funnel, a plastic pipe, a screwdriver, and a few pieces of plumbing were waiting for him.

"Hey Mike, you can come out of the closet now. They're gone."

Michael, hair down to his shoulders, a cautious look on his face, slowly emerged from his hiding spot. The two-person dorm room at Wesleyan University where he'd lived for more than a year was a mess, but it was a deliberate, skillfully constructed mess. Dirty items of clothing were draped like melting clocks across the floor and modest furniture, while books, note pads, and loose papers were scattered around the four corners of the room. It looked almost as though the roommates had been literally beating each other over the head with ideas. Over his bed, Michael had hung an enormous American flag with blue sticky tack. The wall on Danny's side of the room was plastered with posters of old movies he was studying in his classes.

"Them again?"

"Yeah... Listen, Mike, I don't think they're idiots. They obviously know you live here. I keep telling them I don't know you, but they know I'm lying. Why don't you just have it out with them once and for all? It would be better than playing this little game, and we'd finally be left in peace. The guys in the fraternity are starting to get annoyed with your parents being around all the time. It's affecting our credibility."

"If it makes you feel better, I'm not sure I'd call those people my 'parents.'"

"Really? You want to get technical? Mike, this is serious. Getting into Psi Upsilon isn't something to be taken lightly. It's going to open doors for us. You know as well as I do that we're better than everyone else. We're smarter than the little shits we sit next to in class, the ones who still haven't realized they aren't going to get far in life. It's different for us. But being better is pointless if you don't have the status to go with it. So, what you're going to do is call California, tell those people in clear, simple terms not to come here and bother us anymore, and then you're going to help me finish this beer bong so we can give it to the seniors in charge of recruiting."

"I understand what you're saying, but I can't do that."

"Mike, come on, stop acting like a child."

"A child? Come on, Danny. Let's talk about Evelyn for a minute."

Danny's face went pale. His lower jaw jutted out, suggesting he was gritting his teeth.

"Have you forgiven her? If she knocked on the door right now and tried to explain one more time, would you talk to her?"

Danny looked away, frowning. His head moved weakly from right to left, then left to right, then right to left.

"No, you wouldn't. You'd ask me to kick her out. And I'd understand one hundred percent. Same thing if your brother came back to feed you the whole song and dance about how he didn't know you were dating her. You'd want me to tell him to fuck off. Which I've already done and will continue to do for as long as you ask me. You know why? Because you're my friend, Danny. Maybe my best friend. But mainly because it's a question of betrayal, and betrayal is like a stain you just can't wash out. So, imagine that betrayal didn't just have to do with your love life, but with your entire childhood narrative. You probably wouldn't want to talk to the guilty parties, especially if all you stood to gain was maybe getting invited to a few piss-ups."

"You're right, man, I'm sorry. I get it. I was acting like a jerk. Come here."

The two men hugged and gave each other a few slaps on the back.

"I know it's weird to say this between bros, but I love you, Mike."

"I love you too, Danny."

They stepped back, smiling fondly. Danny went over to their mini-fridge.

"Beer?"

"No thanks. I have to focus. I have this thing to finish for Professor Basinger. It'll probably be an all-nighter. Got milk?"

"You and your milk... At least you don't try to repress your mommy issues. You just embrace that shit."

Michael shot him an irritated glance, without any real malice. Danny handed him the plastic gallon jug while he went to grab a can of Old Milwaukee. Michael unscrewed the cap and raised the container in his room-mate's direction.

"Cheers!"

Danny nodded and cracked open the can, which exploded into a fountain of foam. He stood still for a moment, mouth open, covered in sticky liquid. Michael smiled, proud of his little trick.

"You asshole! You shook up the beer again!"

"Take one from the back. I didn't do those."

The student cautiously took another beer out and opened it slowly, reassured by the more moderate hiss. He emptied the contents into a red plastic cup on which he'd written the letters $\Psi\Upsilon$ in black marker.

"Well even if we don't get into the frat, at least I can count on you to make life difficult..."

69

Danny raised his cup to Michael, then downed it in one go, the giant gulp leaving his upper lip crowned with a frothy moustache. Michael stared for a moment at the white moustache, glanced down at his gallon of milk, looked pensive for a second or two, then rushed over to his desk to jot down a few frenzied notes.

IT WAS A SMOOTH FLIGHT to Miami. The air was more humid than in LA. It was just after midnight, but the city was still wide awake. This suited Michael, since he had plans. They were expecting him at Flavor Nightclub in Coconut Grove, a trendy upscale club usually packed with the city's elite. Tonight it was taken over by the members of the *Bad Boys* crew, who'd be filming a scene there over the next few days. The massive club flashed with strobe lights and lasers while industrial music boomed, body shots flowed, and scantily clad black women danced above the crowd in cages suspended from the ceiling. In the VIP lounge, Smith, Lawrence, and Tchéky Karyo sat cross-legged on the floor, listening attentively to Jerry Bruckheimer like diligent students. As Don Simpson looked on silently, the spirited producer was caught up in a lecture on the metaphysics of freedom and, as always, his logic was impeccable. Michael made his way through the dense crowd, nodding affably to a few acquaintances, then came up behind his mentor.

"...which is why in tomorrow's scenes, white women will play the part of sex slaves offered up to our protagonists when they get to the bar, as though this fundamental inversion of the racial hierarchy were to determine even the choice of our filming location. Tomorrow, these poor caged women will be symbolically freed by the sensibility of our smart scouting decision," Bruckheimer was explaining.

"We all know that in the end, it's not those women you want to set free—it's our minds!" Michael cut in, making everyone laugh.

He was greeted warmly and doled out friendly claps on the back to all. The men had already opened, and nearly emptied, several good bottles of ouzo. Everyone was in good spirits.

"I'd like to introduce you to Daphné," said Michael. "She's doing her PhD in film studies at UCLA. We did a seminar together at Wesleyan. She's a delightful young woman."

"Hi, everyone," said Daphné, stepping forward with a radiant smile.

Everyone seemed taken by her. Smith, Lawrence, and Karyo stood up and came to greet her one by one, with charming sincerity. Clearly impressed by the celebrities around her, Daphné tried to catch Bruckheimer's gaze. She didn't think much of him; in fact, she found most of his productions to be, quite frankly, vapid and chauvinistic, but demonstrated her respect and openness by congratulating him on his work. Bruckheimer was the only person who didn't get up to greet her. He smiled politely, but a slight narrowing of his eyes betrayed a glimmer of suspicion, or at least hesitation. He accepted Daphné's compliments nonetheless and slowly began to relax, giving in to reason and drawing on the strength of his logic to fight the purely emotional hostility the young woman inspired in him. "Where are my manners?" he thought, resolving to politely accept the intruder. But just as he began to stand up, he heard an authoritative throat-clearing from the shadows: Don Simpson, silent but all-seeing, did not approve. Having been put in his place, Bruckheimer sat back down and looked away sheepishly, overly conscious of the tension he'd created in the room. He tried in vain to fix his gaze on a detail of the floor, murmured "Nice to meet you," attempting to regain his composure by fiddling with one of his rings as though nothing had happened. No one dared speak for a few moments. It seemed the thermostat had been turned down to sub-zero temperatures while the bass climbed to a deafening volume. Alarmed, Daphné didn't move a muscle. She felt this wasn't just a rejection of her opinions, but rather of her entire being. It was something out of a nightmare.

Michael's brain began to overheat as he racked it for the perfect wisecrack to defuse the situation he was unable to rationalize. The longer he waited, the more he could feel his former classmate's self-esteem dissolve. In the first few nanoseconds of heavy silence, he'd wanted to act the gentleman, letting the woman he actually hardly knew piece together her mangled honor with a biting remark or simple display of indifference, but he now realized her distress and his own responsibility to her. "Ah Jerry, what a charmer! He always has this effect on women," Michael said awkwardly, adding to the tension but managing to crack the thin sheet of ice that had frozen the air in the room. With a forced smile, Michael used the break in silence to take Daphné aside.

"I'm so sorry. I'm not quite sure what just happened."

"My God, they hate me! This is a total disaster. I feel completely humiliated. I've gotta get out of here," she replied, wide-eyed and visibly shaken.

"Listen, wait for me at the bar. Here's a C-note. Order yourself a drink and I'll be there in a minute. I'm going to find out what's going on."

While Daphné disappeared toward the bar, Michael went to talk to the producers. He noticed that Simpson was talking on the phone in a low murmur, which was strange. Michael ignored him and, as usual, addressed Bruckheimer.

"With all due respect, what was that about? What did she ever do to you? That's a really shitty way to treat someone. She's very upset."

"Michael, my dear Michael, it's nothing personal. You know Don has an unusual instinct for these things. You have to trust him. He has come farther than any of us in the quest for ultimate truth. He understands things. His experienced mind analyzes the details of the world with striking precision, uncovering meaning beyond our reach."

"I'm not questioning his intellectual authority. I just want to know... to understand. Because I have the distinct impression that she and I are meant to be together."

"Michael, we would never prevent you from doing anything. We're simply here to offer guidance, counsel. You're still free to do whatever you want. But in our opinion she doesn't belong here. She doesn't have the necessary sensibility. But if your heart tells you differently..."

"How can you say that she lacks sensibility? You don't even know her!"

Bruckheimer didn't respond, preferring to stay silent.

"I admit that we've had our artistic differences, but debate is a good thing. It stimulates the mind, forces us to call things into question and take into account all sides of the equation. She makes me feel alive, makes me feel..."

Michael didn't have the luxury of finishing his sentence. He was interrupted by a sharp cry. It was Daphné. She was screaming for help in the midst of the trance-like crowd as two muscular men, who seemed more like kidnappers than security, dragged her violently toward the exit. His senses heightened by the urgency of the moment, Michael managed to keep his eyes on the men and saw that they were armed with machine guns. Without thinking, he jumped the low VIP lounge wall and landed on one of the speakers on the floor below. "Daphné!" he cried, trying to push through the crowd that was innocently but persistently blocking his way. "Daphné!" he cried again, getting a "Michael!" in response. He was slightly disoriented by the strobe lights, and from the middle of the dance floor he was finding it difficult to keep the exit sign in sight as he struggled toward it, determined to put an end to this baffling situation and return Daphné to safety. "Michael!" she cried again, throwing feeble punches at her assailants, who were yelling at her in a foreign language. A well-aimed kick got one of them right in the balls, incapacitating him. Now was her chance: with one hand free, she wrested herself from the second man's grasp during the confusion and pushed her way into the crowd to find Michael. He had witnessed her escape and quickened his pace, only to be unexpectedly and brutally intercepted by a powerful punch in the face delivered by an unknown fist. Michael fell to the ground, knocking into a few clubbers and stirring up more of a commotion. A space opened up, forming an improvised ring in the middle of the mostly disinterested crowd. In front of Michael stood a man about his height, but more muscular and with a resolute stare. Michael was not aggressive by nature, but he was pragmatic and he knew the stakes: to protect Daphné, he would have to defeat this criminal in hand-to-hand combat. In an almost cartoonish mix of determination and clumsiness, Daphné continued to gain ground as she elbowed her way through the dancers. Michael stared down his adversary and took advantage of the few seconds before the official start of hostilities to search his soul; he calmly recalled his years of training, a good part of which had been spent learning the rudiments of fighting. His father, before the betrayal, had walked him through the process, from (surprisingly technical) childish roughhousing to armed clashes. This humanistic tutelage had left him well prepared. But he had yet to apply the concepts in a hostile setting, which precluded utter confidence in his abilities. When his adversary rushed at him, Michael dodged him, responding with a straight right to the jaw before pulling him into a bear hug. The criminal was caught off guard, but quickly recovered, compensating for his technical disadvantage with multiple elbow blows to Michael's ribs. Michael yielded, released his grip, and was hit with a powerful uppercut. Everything momentarily went dark. He felt his opponent moving away and came to, reactivated by the adrenaline. His stocky adversary had only retreated to grab a beer bottle, which he now brandished as he charged toward Michael. At that moment, another strident "Michael!" pierced the bassline; Daphné, now about ten feet away, had just been seized by a fourth kidnapper and was being dragged back toward the exit, this time more successfully. Michael let his muscle memory take over, his mind taking a back seat and watching the scene from outside his body. His left fist quickly struck the inside of the attacker's right wrist, hitting the nerves in his forearm and causing him to release the bottle. Michael drew his fingers together in perfect form and hit the man's chest in three points, paralyzing him in a grotesque position. Then, in a fluid motion that made every step of his attack appear as one single, graceful movement, Michael neutralized the man, sending him flying back against the wall and into a huge built-in aquarium, which shattered dramatically and flooded the room with water that reeked of plants, of life.

ON A PENCHANT FOR SCIENCE

AS A YOUTH, Michael was more than a burgeoning intellectual with the sole objective of gaining a better theoretical understanding of the world around him; he also had a strong desire for movement, to take action in the visible realm, which he satisfied by spending long hours experimenting in the backyard of the modern and impressively large white house, testing the basic laws of physics and chemistry that filled the pages of the kids' science magazines littering his den floor. Sometimes alone, sometimes as his parents looked on in amusement, Michael would spend whole afternoons setting up rudimentary installations that could move the theoretical beyond the abstract to create a concrete force of action. Which is how, between the ages of six and twelve, he was able to confirm—albeit with varying degrees of success—the soundness of the laws of Newton, Avogadro, Hooke, Joule and Gay-Lussac, Kepler, and Archimedes, to name a few.

Enthusiastic about her son's curiosity but fearing time would blur these precious memories, Harriett

decided one crisp grey summer day in 1976 to purchase a Super 8 movie camera, with which she began
capturing on film the furtive moments that enhanced
her day-to-day role as a mother. Michael, intrigued by
the enormous reassurance this device seemed to offer
the person he considered responsible for his arrival
in the world, and driven by a propensity for discovery,
immediately wanted to know how it worked. He was
familiar with the wonders of movie-making, having
visited the San Fernando Valley cinema twice weekly
for years—a near-sacred ritual for the Bay family—
and thereby becoming acquainted with the poetry of
Welles, Chaplin, Kubrick, Renoir, Truffaut, Forman, and
Kurosawa. He began to use the new tool straightaway,
never imagining the important role it would soon play
in the quest for meaning that would shape his entire
life. Not wishing to dampen her son's natural enthusiasm or jeopardize his future (she had been recently
studying psychoanalytic criticism, a field of research
she quickly abandoned, disenchanted by its minimal
effect on her ability to interpret texts), Harriett agreed,
albeit reluctantly, to let Michael use her precious movie
camera, her insurance policy on their memories. Thus,
young Michael was allowed to discover the fascinating
possibilities offered by cinematographic language, so
long as those first formal narrative experiences took
place under Harriett's close but caring supervision.
Jim was especially strict regarding Michael's use of the
camera, seeing it as an opportunity for Michael to learn

to respect the rules and the fragility of things. Under no circumstances was the movie camera to be used without adult supervision, failing which there would be consequences. What they were remained unclear, but simply alluding to them—again, Jim's idea—seemed a sufficient deterrent. The couple thought it best to add a second precautionary measure: the film, the camera's very reason for being, was always kept hidden from the boy. Michael, who considered his work more important than the need to respect questionable rules, was thus forced to be resourceful.

Maintaining the modern and impressively large white house was a sizable task for two professionals with demanding schedules. Despite this, the Bays, who had always believed that hiring a cleaning lady would only sustain the utterly unjustifiable dynamic of cultural subordination whereby rich American homeowners continued to perpetuate their ancestral legacy of possession, attempted as best they could to keep the family home as welcoming as possible in order to foster relaxation, reflection, and mental well-being. This is how Michael came up with the idea of offering, in exchange for a sum that was modest but that sufficiently acknowledged his efforts, to actively participate in the daily household chores. For several weeks, he scrubbed the floors, cut the grass (riding the lawn tractor added a certain enjoyment to the job), pruned the rose bushes, cleaned the mirrors, polished the appliances, and filed the bills, all tasks he approached with seriousness and diligence. After having saved more than a hundred dollars in two months, Michael went to town to buy tractor fuel at his father's request, using the opportunity to make a secret stop at the local photo store. He described his mother's camera model and the main objectives of his film shoot to the store clerk in great detail, and returned home satisfied, a can of two-stroke engine oil in his right hand and numerous feet of Super 8mm film in his bag, well hidden under a grease-covered LA Dodgers t-shirt.

The following afternoon while his parents were out at work, Michael put into play his most ambitious cinematic-science project to date. Eager to discover the coefficient by which the speed of an object in motion would be multiplied when propelled by lit gunpowder, he decided to use the electric train he had received for his sixth birthday and some firecrackers—not yet possessing the skills to make his own powder and fuse—from the neighborhood 7-Eleven. Out behind the modern and impressively large white house, Michael set up the miniature tracks in a straight line about sixty feet long to serve as a runway, placed the train on the tracks, and used industrial-strength tape to secure a dozen small explosives linked together by a single fuse in the driver's compartment. He loaded his mother's Super 8 with the film cartridge he'd obtained earlier and, excited to finally record his experiments on film, he turned on the devices, lit the fuse and, for the first time in his life, called out, "Action!"

As soon as it was switched on, the train began to advance steadily along the makeshift ramp, unaware of the spectacular fate that awaited it. His right eye comfortably pressed against the viewfinder, Michael fit the entire scene into the frame (as per his scientific methodology), fighting the visceral urge to get in closer to the action and capture every possible angle. And while at that precise moment, the sunlight appeared in premeditated perfection, flooding the image with the kind of Southern heat that makes you long for a Coke, while the American flag his parents had proudly hung in the yard flapped in the background inspiring bravery and humility, while he heard somewhere deep within him the glorious notes of a military anthem, adding a touch of grandeur and greatness to his role of lone director, Michael Bay was suddenly struck by the inevitable: next to the rail tracks, just ten feet from the designated point of explosion, sat the can of two-stroke engine oil. There was no time to react: a fraction of a second before meeting the firebomb, the locomotive, rather than being propelled forward, was annihilated by a loud and powerful detonation, sending pieces of white-hot plastic flying twenty feet from the detonation point and almost immediately igniting the gas can. A huge, billowing cloud of fire and gas vapor instantly filled the backyard and rose into the San Fernando Valley skies, causing the temperature of the air surrounding Michael, a stunned expression on his angelic little face, to spike and prompting dogs to start barking nervously and neighborhood cleaning ladies to shout colorful Latino expressions, threatening everything and everyone.

Trembling and shaken to the very core, Michael stood rooted to the spot for several minutes, staring blankly, distractedly listening to the sound of approaching sirens. The Los Angeles firefighters gracefully descended on the scene as though moving in slow motion, dragging their impressive hoses and skillfully extinguishing the hundred or so tiny fires calmly raging in the backyard. A firefighter came over to Michael and began asking questions that he couldn't understand, that seemed warped by his own stupor, then helped him over to safety near the pool. Michael's complete shutdown prompted everyone who tried, in vain, to communicate with him to conclude that the boy was in shock, despite the fact that Michael was not particularly frightened nor had his hearing been impaired by the blast. Sitting in a plastic lawn chair, a blanket draped over his shoulders, all Michael Bay could think of was the little tea-soaked madeleine that had plunged Proust's narrator into a troubling state of remembrance; while his memories were nothing but images of harmonious family life, at that moment, for the first time, he recalled the events of March 19, 1967, the day he had been taken home by a mother and father who were not his own. He had never once suspected he'd been adopted. His confidence had been betrayed. The explosion had ignited within him the question of his origins.

ON POTASSIUM PERMANGANATE

DAPHNÉ HAD BEEN DRAGGED out back. As he arrived breathless in the club parking lot, Michael noted what a beautiful night it was. His keen eye scanned the area and quickly spotted Daphné, who cried out his name one last time before she was bundled into the backseat of a car, which took off at full speed, leaving two rubbery black stripes on the asphalt. Michael was overcome by conflicting emotions that excited his sense of nuance: true, he was upset to see Daphné taken, due to his own actions, beyond his reach to a seemingly fateful end, but he was also thrilled to the very core by the imminence of a car chase. To make up for the already substantial distance between him and the fleeing car, Michael took out his chrome-plated nine-millimeter and aimed for one of the back tires, holding his breath as he pulled the trigger. He watched the bullet miss its mark, hit the hubcap, and send a burst of sparks flying. Will Smith and Martin Lawrence suddenly appeared at his side, ready to back him up. With not a moment to lose, the three men jumped into the nearest vehicle, which happened to be a *Bad Boys* production truck. Michael took the wheel, relieved that the key was already in the ignition—not that he couldn't hotwire a car, but every second counted. He hit the gas. In the distance the kidnapper's vehicle took a right and disappeared around a corner. Fortunately, Michael had taken an active role in scouting the location just a few weeks earlier, inspired by a newfound interest in wetland urbanism. As a result he had excellent knowledge of the neighborhood and its back streets, giving him a distinct strategic advantage. And strategy was needed if he hoped to come out victorious in the chase: the converted ice cream truck being used to transport film equipment was a poor match for the kidnappers' powerful, gleaming, moss green 5.2L V8 Jeep Grand Cherokee.

When the ice cream truck got to the street the Jeep had taken, Michael kept going straight, knowing there was a diagonal shortcut that would, according to his calculations, set them ahead. Michael's plan was doubly advantageous, as it also meant the swarthy kidnappers, no longer seeing anyone in pursuit, would naturally slow so as to avoid drawing attention from the law and arrive at their destination undetected. The truck sped through the night, Miami's neon lights, luxury cars, prominent midriffs, and breast implants zooming by at a frenetic speed. Adrenaline pumping through their veins, the three men hadn't felt so alive or dedicated to a mission since they had read *The Wretched of the Earth* together.

"Now seems like the perfect time to test this," said Michael after a moment of silence. As the traffic grew lighter, with one hand on the wheel and an eye on the road, he dug into his pocket for a cassette tape, which he put into the stereo. "It's the preliminary soundtrack for the film. Mark Mancina sent it to me a couple days ago."

A powerful combination of brass, electric guitar, and fast-paced percussion with subtle tribal undertones rang out in the truck, urging them forward. As the volume rose, Smith, Lawrence, and Michael yelled to each other ever louder over the music, testosterone pumping as it vied for full control of their actions.

"I hope you know what you're doing," bellowed Lawrence, "'cause it's starting to look like we've lost them for good."

"Trust me. I know what I'm doing."

"Can't you go any faster?" Smith yelled. "A car chase in an ice cream truck—seriously? What were you thinking?"

"I didn't have time to think."

"Time to think?" cried Smith. "That's a first! I thought you were more Cartesian than that! What's going on? That girl take away your ability to think rationally?"

"Seems like Mr. Simpson was right," Lawrence heaped on. "Bringing women into the picture is always a bad idea. She's not our problem. We should let her sort this out herself!"

Their comments cut Michael to the quick.

"Chill out, both of you!" he barked, turning to look at them. "I'm the one who convinced her to come to Miami with us, so I'm responsible for her! I don't remember anyone forcing you to get in the truck!"

"Watch out!" shouted Lawrence, pointing to a giant tractor trailer blocking the intersection ahead as they approached at high speed.

They hung on tight as Michael cranked the wheel to the right, the ice cream truck jerking into a reluctant turn. Acting on instinct alone, the vigilant but inexperienced tractor trailer driver slammed on the brakes and wheeled hard to the left. The vehicle skidded forward and the truck cab veered out into the heavy stream of oncoming traffic while the trailer, which had broken away, swayed and lurched toward Bay, Smith, and Lawrence. As the ice cream truck turned, its wheels lost their grip on the asphalt, overpowered by the centrifugal force. The music reached a crescendo as they hurtled toward the trailer, whose left wheels began to lift off the ground. Inside the ice cream truck, the men exchanged a brief yet intense look of horror. Michael's only thought—perhaps his very last—was of Daphné. Beautiful Daphné, who'd made him feel something he'd never felt before. Maybe it was the particular drama of their current situation, but he felt a pang of sadness and realized that he loved her. There it was; he loved her. To hell with those faint-of-hearts for whom such an admission comes only after long months of evaluation, calculation, and hesitation. Sure, he barely knew her, but he realized love wasn't a rational conclusion; he couldn't explain *why* he felt this way, but for one of the first times in his life, he didn't need to understand. About six feet before the vehicles' point of impact, he felt peace, comfort, and even a brief twinge of happiness.

By some fortuitous turn of events, the ice cream truck and the trailer collided perfectly parallel to each other. Michael's vehicle suffered only minor damage and when it skidded to a halt, sat facing the busy street ahead that was—conveniently—the route he'd been planning to take. The trailer wasn't so lucky; already unstable, it absorbed the full impact of the collision and began teetering in the other direction, crashing down onto a row of parked cars. Amid the sound of crumpling metal, car alarms, and panicked cries, the ice cream truck drove off in hot pursuit, its passengers relieved to be alive.

"What's that smell?" asked Michael, sniffing loudly.

"I don't know," said Smith, "but it stinks."

"I think it's coming from the back of the truck," added Lawrence, looking back at the cargo. "What is that?"

About twenty enormous barrels wobbled dangerously behind them.

"What's written on them?" asked Michael.

"$KMnO_4$... Anybody know what that is?" Lawrence replied.

Michael sighed, visibly upset.

"What... What?! What's going on?" demanded Smith.

The ice cream truck was speeding past the other cars in the lane; Michael had to concentrate and keep calm if he wanted to pass them without inflicting too much damage. He did his best, but nonetheless swiped a few side mirrors, which exploded into thousands of gleaming shards.

"It's potassium permanganate. Production uses it to develop film. It works well when it's diluted with water and mixed with potassium carbonate or sodium hydroxide. It was also used to make camera flashes back in the day. But in such a large quantity and under our current conditions, well, I'm not sure how to put this... but there's an extremely high risk of explosion."

"Explosion?!" yelled Lawrence. "So what you're saying is we're zigzagging in and out of traffic at seventy-five miles an hour in a goddamm bomb on wheels?!"

Panic-stricken, Will Smith burst into tears.

"It'll be fine. We just have to be careful."

Michael, concentrating hard, jerked the wheel sharply to the right to avoid the traffic blocking all four lanes several feet ahead. The ice cream truck squeezed between a row of parked cars and a fire truck, trailing two rows of sparks on either side, like the flare of Bengal lights. Instead of slowing down, Michael sped up.

The ice cream truck arrived at the intersection where, according to Michael's calculations, they should cross paths with the Jeep. Michael slowed down to blend in. Smith and Lawrence looked around for their target. Michael spotted the Jeep straight ahead, three blocks down. He accelerated gently, so as not to warn them of his approach; after all, the kidnappers might not have even noticed they were being tailed. With a series of skillful maneuvers, Michael managed to bring the truck up alongside the Jeep, maintaining a speed of around thirty miles per hour.

"She's alone in the back seat," Smith pointed out.

"Take the wheel!" Michael shouted to Lawrence. "Keep driving and I'll try to get her attention."

Michael and Martin Lawrence switched spots. Michael discreetly tried to catch Daphné's eye, counting on the same magnetism that had seemed to unite them since their chance encounter in a Los Angeles bookstore a few hours earlier. Daphné spotted him through the window and felt a mix of apprehension and relief. Michael looked so handsome and heroic in the ice cream truck's side window. He motioned with his eyes that she should move behind the passenger seat, that he was going to attempt something. Lawrence gradually closed the gap between the two vehicles, and when the Jeep's back window was perfectly lined up with his center of gravity, Michael shattered it with a powerful kick. Surprised, the kidnappers began to yell and accelerated, but Lawrence proved to be a skillful driver and managed to keep the ice cream truck more or less directly aligned with the busted window.

"Grab on to my belt and hold tight!" Michael yelled to Will Smith, who did as he was told.

Once more making sure to lock eyes with Daphné, Michael let himself fall toward her, grabbing hold of the edge of her window and bridging the two vehicles, which were now speeding along at a tense eighty miles per hour on a minor Miami boulevard. Michael held fast and redoubled his efforts, managing to climb shoulder-deep into the Jeep with Smith still holding fast to his belt. The risky maneuver attracted the attention of the kidnapper in the passenger seat, who, shouting in a language Michael couldn't decipher, grabbed his gun, turned around, and pointed it at him. From the backseat Daphné saw a gun appear between the two front seats, the first she'd ever seen in real life, which heightened her panic. Despite her emotional state, she had the presence of mind to deliver a forceful kick to the criminal's hand, knocking the gun to the floor. Michael used the diversion to put his plan into action: he grabbed hold of Daphné's arms, pulled her toward him, checked his grip, and called to Lawrence to quickly fall back to the left, leaving his fate in the hands of his belt, as they were yanked backward. The whole thing was surreal, especially for Daphné who, for a few seconds, seemed to float helplessly in the air, the asphalt moving beneath her at breakneck speed. As if by magic she yielded, accepting her lack of control with a certain calm, tenderly losing herself in the comfort of Michael's gaze, which was completely at odds with Smith's panicked expression. Then with a sharp tug, Smith managed to pull the duo into the relative safety of the ice cream truck.

"It's going to be okay," Michael whispered into Daphné's ear. "It's all over."

Was he really that optimistic or was he simply trying to reassure her? Whatever the case, he had no time to think about it. The kidnappers were clearly not the type to give up so easily. The driver of the Jeep ramped up the aggression, slamming into the left side of the truck, gouging its side, and running it off the road.

"Shit!" yelled Lawrence. "If they knew they were going to blow us all up, they wouldn't be doing that!"

"Blow us all up?" Daphné asked nervously. "What's he talking about?"

The truck was silent, aside from the still-frenetic sounds of Mark Mancina's score.

"What's he talking about?!" Daphné asked again.

"I don't want to worry you," answered Bay, "but I think all those cans behind us are filled with an explosive. But really, don't worry. Martin is an excellent driver. He'll get us out of this. Right, Martin?"

Daphné was speechless, emotionally incapable of reacting to the news.

"Fuck you, man!" replied Lawrence, as he avoided another swipe by the Jeep. "The truck was *your* idea. Don't you put this on me. *You* get us out of this shitstorm!"

"Turn down here. Now!"

Lawrence took the next left, tires screeching, ignoring the pile of construction materials in the way. The ice cream truck had no trouble smashing through the few wood barricades obstructing access to the work site and, for a moment, the sudden change in direction proved lifesaving. The kidnappers, surprised by the maneuver, continued straight down the boulevard. Everyone took a breath, choosing to ignore the unlikely odds that they could be in the clear so easily. There was something bleak and disquieting about the road they had turned onto. It was still unpaved, providing little grip for the tires, and its deep, barely visible crevices made driving perilous. With the road still unlit and the truck's head-lights damaged, their only light was the almost-full moon, which painted their tense expressions with a dim bluish glow.

The scene suddenly lit up. Behind them they could see the bright lights of the Jeep accelerating toward them, the terrain giving it the upper hand. Then, they heard a series of loud pops. Not only were the kidnap-pers relentless, but now they were upping the stakes with a spray of machine gun fire targeting the ice cream truck and its barrels of potassium permanganate. Who the hell were they? And why were they so interested in sweet Daphné, whose erratic breathing suggested that she was on the verge of passing out? True, Michael barely knew her. His analysis of the situation, conducted almost unconsciously and in the heat of the moment, was therefore lacking certain parameters. Perhaps she was from a rich family and the kidnappers were merely seeking a generous ransom. Perhaps, just like the female lead in *Bad Boys*, she had witnessed a crime—maybe even a murder!—and they were trying to take her out. Or per-haps—no doubt—they had just mistaken her for someone else. Whatever the case, before looking for answers, they had to deal with the problem at hand, especially now that a second and third volley of shots had rung out, making Lawrence's driving increasingly erratic.

"Shit, shit, shit!" yelled Will Smith. "We're all gonna die! This is it! We're all gonna die!"

"Where's your gun?" Lawrence shouted at Michael, clumsily swerving to avoid an enormous crater revealing a portion of the city's water supply system.

Michael reluctantly considered the possibility of contributing to the gunfire.

"I don't know... I shot at them without thinking before. It was just to slow them down. But now... There are real lives at stake... I don't know, guys. This isn't the movies. There are going to be real consequences..."

"Michael!" interrupted Lawrence. "It's us or them! It's that simple!"

Another two rounds rang out. Nobody noticed that Daphné had passed out. Michael grabbed his gun, stuck his head and one arm out the truck door, and, after a brief hesitation, squeezed the trigger, only to miss the target completely.

"It's my left hand!" Michael apologized. "And the headlights are blinding me. It's hard!"

Michael fired again, with the same result. In his defense, Lawrence's wild driving was not conducive to straight shooting.

"The road! The road! Stop! Do something!" It was Lawrence, louder this time.

Several hundred yards in front of the ice cream truck stood an imposing cement barrier surrounded by heavy machinery. There was no doubt the impact would be fatal. Michael froze. He looked at Daphné lying on the floor of the truck, strangely peaceful. Smith and Lawrence's cries, though deafening, failed to reach him. Michael felt an aqueous heat rise up inside him and he couldn't keep his jaw from trembling. He let himself fall to his knees, took Daphné's head in his hands, and brought it to his chest in a protective gesture he knew was ultimately futile.

Just then, a pothole in the road swallowed one of the ice cream truck's tires, propelling the truck to the side and causing the back doors to swing open. The Jeep's blinding headlights illuminated the truck's interior, pulling Smith out of his daze. For a fraction of a second, the glow sent him back to the set of the *Fresh Prince of Bel-Air* and the exhilarating power he used to feel with the spotlight on him. Though he had just been starting out, he'd known he had what it took to be a star, one whose talents alone would make or break his future films. He would have to get used to taking things into his own hands. He would have to embrace his destiny as leading man. Keenly aware of the imminent impact with the concrete barrier, Smith grabbed the gun from Michael—who put up no resistance—tucked it momentarily into the waistband of his pants, then moved to the back of the truck and, with a strength that surprised even himself, heaved several barrels of potassium permanganate out onto the bumpy road. Hampered by the unforeseen obstacles, the kidnappers slowed and swerved like clumsy slalom skiers to avoid the barrels, but continued their relentless pursuit. Smith grabbed the nine-millimeter and, eyes ablaze, let out a protracted battle cry and emptied the round in the kidnappers' direction, hitting one of the barrels near the Jeep and setting off an impressive whitish explosion that flipped the vehicle on its side. Smith had little time to admire his stunningly destructive work before he was sent flying backward—not by the languorous wave of heat generated by the explosion, but because Lawrence had slammed on the brakes, bringing the truck to a screaming halt only inches from the concrete barrier. Lawrence sat motion-less for a few seconds, his arms still fully locked as he gripped the wheel, eyes closed and teeth clenched, then he slowly opened his eyes, looked around him without moving a muscle, made sure they were out of danger, and let out a noise mid-way between a sigh of relief and a sob. He ejected the tape from the stereo, the only sound now the crackling flames next to the ice cream truck.

Fully entwined with Daphné on the truck floor, Michael felt a strange sensation. While facing probable death he had devoted his entire self to protecting the girl, but the power and proximity of the explosion had sent him into a trance-like state, filling him with a strong yet fleeting sensation: he saw himself as an infant, pro-tected from the world by tanned arms, his head comfort-ably resting on a soft, ample bosom. Almost as quickly, Michael was brought back to reality.

"Michael? Michael! What's going on? You're hurting me!" said Daphné, who had just come to, roused by Michael's arms tightening around her and now confronted by his rapid breathing and the disturbing look in his glassy stare.

The fleeting moments of comfort had already slipped away, a vague and unreachable memory. Troubled but once again in control, he let go of her and smiled.

"Everything's alright, Daphné. It's over. You're safe now."

The four of them filed out of the truck to get a better look at the scene down the street. The barrel was still burning and its violet flames had engulfed the underside of the Jeep, which was still resting on its left side, the windows completely shattered. In the distance, sirens from various emergency vehicles grew louder. A local TV station helicopter circled the site, aiming a powerful spotlight at the Jeep as it captured the scene on film. Below, no longer in the dark, they could make out something moving inside the burning vehicle. The outline of a bloody hand covered in glass shards emerged from where the windshield had been, as one of the kidnappers pulled himself halfway out of the Jeep. Michael, profoundly disturbed by the seemingly absurd events of the last half-hour, took advantage of the man's vulnerable state to search for answers.

"Who are you?! *Qui êtes-vous*?! *Chi siete*?! *Кто вы*?!"

Not getting a response and hampered by the sound of the helicopter and sirens, Michael took a few steps closer to the kidnapper and repeated his question. He even attempted a translation into Arabic, though he was somewhat unsure of his pronunciation.

"Who are you?! *Qui êtes-vous*?! *Chi siete*?! *Кто вы*?! من أنت؟"

Their eyes met. Michael was surprised to note that there was not a trace of ill will in his expression. Slowly and with great difficulty, the man lifted his arm and pointed toward the group. He finally spoke, uttering something incomprehensible in a hoarse voice, something that sounded like "*Peristasmoz!*"

"What?! *Quoi*?!" asked Michael.

"*Peristas...*"

The man's response was cut off by another violent explosion; this time it was the Jeep's gas tank. With it went any chance of an explanation. Michael lost his footing and fell backward, more out of surprise than from the (very real) change in air pressure. Tailbone throbbing, he gingerly got to his feet, the others still several yards away, and once again felt a shift in consciousness. But the feeling paled in comparison with what he had felt as he lay on the ice cream truck floor with Daphné clasped against his chest. Like a heroin addict trying in vain, dose after dose, to relive the state of grace of that first hit, he felt betrayed by the lesser effects of his high. He closed his eyes, furrowed his brow, and concentrated as hard as he could, using willpower alone, trying to chase the strange sensation of truth that had left him so quickly. What he would give to feel the calm of those golden arms again, but most of all to see a face, or even just a feature, that might allow him to delve back into the depths of his memory and reconnect with the image of his unknown, mysterious, displaced mother. Michael was so wrapped up in his thoughts, so determined to force an introspection, albeit one triggered by external stimuli, that he barely noticed his frightened friends waving frantically to warn him that several barrels, knocked over by the gas tank explosion, were rolling menacingly toward the burning Jeep. It was a physical sensation that helped him snap out of it, if only momentarily. Goosebumps—a purely epidermal expression of emotion—covered his skin and he felt the delicate down on his arms come alive, curling and swaying in the waves of intense heat created by the successive and practically choreographed explosion of six barrels lighting up the night like camera flashes. Rather than run and take shelter, Michael stood tall and welcomed the scene, the same way he had twenty-seven years ago, the day Harriett rescued him on the side of a white-hot California highway. And perhaps it was because of the potassium permanganate, which was after all used to process film, but Michael himself was processing something, reaching a sort of revelation or epiphany, in that the only smell he was able to make out besides the irritating, nauseating gas fumes that permeated the air was the scent of orange blossoms. Since the uniformly concrete backdrop against which he was playing both spectator and actor was devoid of vegetation, the persistent yet sweet perfume, which he found almost invasive, could only be from his puzzling past, a clue to help him decode the mystery of his origin. He suddenly felt himself in another time and space, closer than he had ever been to the place of his early childhood—his true childhood. Despite the time that had since passed, he still hadn't forgiven Jim and Harriett for not having been honest from the start, for having taken advantage of his naivety to use him as some sort of accessory or unwilling actor in their egotistical fantasy of parenthood. While he could not deny that it had benefited him to a certain extent, growing up as he had in an environment that nurtured his mind, that was a different matter altogether. This was about betrayal, or rather, about truth. How could he know who he really was without knowing where he came from? Jim and Harriett refused to shed light on the subject, and so long as they continued to profess their ignorance—whether in earnest or in an attempt to shield him (it made no difference)—Michael continued to ignore their repeated attempts at reconciliation. What he wanted to know right now was where that cerebral bergamot scent was coming from, a scent that was already being overcome by the pungent, more imminent smell of burnt tires and hair. The euphoric effect of the chemical explosions was beginning to wear off and Michael realized he wouldn't get a clear answer that humid evening in Miami. One thing did, however, become clear: if he reacted this intensely to huge explosions—which he felt were, above all, explosions of meaning—he should make them the basis for his poetic art. He would strive, film after film, to reproduce such detonations, in the hopes of unshrouding his mysterious beginnings. Overcome by both a lack of fulfillment and sense of enthusiasm for the future, as the TV helicopter above was buffeted by the fireballs flying in its direction, noisily approaching with the hope of capturing a few faces on film, Michael Bay stood up, turned toward the ice cream truck, and opened his arms to Daphné, who flew into them and thanked him for saving her life, told him he was her hero, and, for the very first time, as Martin Lawrence and Will Smith looked on with a complicit smile, kissed him passionately in the midst of the inferno.

ON YEARS OF LEARNING

FROM 1982 TO 1986, Michael attended Wesleyan University, a private post-secondary institution specializing in the arts and sciences, located in Middletown, Connecticut, more than twenty-eight hundred miles from the San Fernando Valley where he had grown up. To Michael's mind (following extensive reading during his adolescent years), philosophy was not a science that one could master—or even gain a working knowledge of—in the classroom; preferring to carry out his quest for meaning alone, with only the true masters as his guide, eternalized in their writing, he opted for an undergraduate education in English and film. A brilliant yet restless student, Michael studied and was particularly interested in the examination of identity in Shohei Imamura's films, the influence of Nouveau Roman narrative techniques in *Last Year at Marienbad*, Porter's aesthetic of the tableau, the poetry and temporal relationships in Tarkovsky's *Stalker*, the ethical dilemmas raised by Serge Doubrovsky's fiction, and the post-colonial discourse in Conrad's *Heart of Darkness*, and was also one of the first to note the ground-breaking theoretical importance of French philosopher Gilles Deleuze's *The Movement Image*. It was in fact in relation to this text (and, two years later, to *The Time-Image*) that Michael met Jeanine Basinger, the film historian generally credited with bringing Wesleyan's film program international acclaim. Excited by her student's expansive, original ideas, Basinger soon took Michael under her wing; in addition to introducing him to her entourage of scholars and artists, she asked him to join her research group at the time, which was studying the question of genre in World War II films[*]—an offer he readily accepted. This inspiring intellectual relationship was not, however, enough to convince him, once he had graduated and proven himself, to set up for good on the East Coast, where a brilliant university career was not just a promise, but a certainty. Driven by a juvenile desire to get away from the theoretical for a while to pursue the practical, Michael enrolled several weeks later at Art Center College of Design in the heart of Pasadena, which boasted a solid reputation for churning out creative film professionals and technicians and where, until 1989, Michael strove to new heights in the graduate film

---

[*] The fruit of this research group's work to which Bay contributed appeared in 1986 under the title *The World War II Combat Film: Anatomy of a Genre*, New York, Columbia University Press, 373 p. An updated and expanded edition of the book was published in 2003 by Wesleyan University Press.

production program, earning the film studies equivalent of a master's in creative writing. Back in California, just a couple miles from the little community of Hidden Hills, home to the modern and impressively large white house, Michael still refused to speak to the people who'd raised him in an illusion of legitimacy, having not yet found it within himself to rebuild ties which, after dramatically deteriorating following the electric-train incident, had been completely severed when he moved to Connecticut. From that point on, his work would be his life. Just one week after obtaining his Art Center degree, Michael was recruited by the powerful and much-respected Propaganda Films and, at the age of twenty-four, directed his first commercial.

Despite the industry's apparent recognition of his talent, Michael, humble and methodical, believed making commercials (and soon after, big-budget music videos) to be more of a continuation of his academic career—or his formal education at least—rather than its validation, which was not something he subscribed to anyway. He sought, above all, through base commercial means, to refine the poetry of his art. Initially hesitant to work for multinationals who exploited human rights—he'd begun reading Chomsky—Michael first took a job for the American Red Cross, convinced that his creation would help promote balance in the world (or at least it would be a start). It was, in fact, a start that the industry received favorably. Excited at the prospect of a distinctive, illuminating new voice among its ranks, they awarded him a prestigious Clio straight away, a prize that was normally an end-of-career goal. Michael then received a slew of offers. Coca-Cola was the most insistent (the big guns had already begun to associate Bay's refreshing aesthetic with their product). At first disgusted at the idea of contributing to the icon of capitalism's barbaric spread, he was tempted when they sweetened the pot, offering total creative freedom and an additional one hundred thousand dollars. He looked at the positive side: still passionate about representations of World War II, an interest he'd developed under the tutelage of Jeanine Basinger, Michael believed this was an opportunity (and the means) to finally create a large-scale mini-movie based exclusively on the conclusions of his former research group, whose devotion he longed for more and more each day. He planned to use the money to start a rare book collection, still bitter about missing his chance at a signed copy of *Идиот* that one of the small bookshops he frequented had in stock for a short time, though he was too poverty-stricken to buy it back then. After finishing the project (it had, in the end, been inspired by the iconic work of photographer Alfred Eisenstaedt capturing the victorious return of navy officers with one romantic snapshot), he was hired by the California Milk Processor Board in 1993 to come up with a nationwide campaign that would give milk back its former glory. Thanks to his famous *Got Milk?* campaign, Michael became a top-tier commercial director who'd been able to capture the hearts of the masses with a spot that relied, interestingly enough, on high-brow references (Austrian chamber music, the famous duel between eighteenth-century American politicians Alexander Hamilton and Aaron Burr, a relatable representation of the intellectual). The commercial was not only a resounding success with the general public, but won the Grand Prix Clio for Commercial of the Year and made it into MoMA's permanent collection. Michael followed this up with a whole host of contracts, more than a hundred in all—for Nike, Budweiser, Reebok, Miller, Victoria's Secret, Chevrolet, and others—that he saw as opportunities to experiment. In 1994, at age twenty-eight, Michael Bay was named Commercial Director of the Year by the Directors Guild of America, making him the youngest director to have received practically every award in advertising—a record he still holds today.

ON CELIBACY

IF HE HADN'T BEEN A MOVIE GUY HIMSELF, Michael might have believed what happened to him the day of the premiere had been staged.

An habitual early riser, Michael was flipping briskly through his various daily newspapers when he was interrupted by his "Star-Spangled Banner" ringtone. Hot California sunlight spilled into the generously fenestrated apartment, creating an effect akin to certain William Turner paintings. It was not all that surprising to be receiving a call this early; after all, in just a few hours Michael's directorial debut would be released to the world as a handful of stars walked the red carpet of the Chinese Theater to see Will Smith and Martin Lawrence incarnate the ideas of Césaire, Fanon, Memmi, and Berque. No doubt it was an assistant calling, overwhelmed with last-minute preparations.

"Mr. Bay? This is Detective Hummel, Miami PD. I'm calling regarding our investigation into the events of last January."

They had been as of yet unable to discover the identity of Daphné's kidnappers. Blatantly disregarding the film company doctor's advice, Michael had foregone the several days of rest prescribed, not wanting to delay shooting and insistent on funneling the adrenaline rush he'd gotten from the car chase into his work. He'd even been inspired to add a scene based on the real-life events into the film, with Columbia's insurance benefits covering the over-budget expenditures. Though he was deeply perturbed by the mysterious criminals' motivations, he trusted the local police to do their jobs and, after providing a detailed and stylistically impeccable statement, he waited for a significant breakthrough.

"I have to say, it's a pretty strange case. I don't want to bore you with the technical details—I know you're a busy man. I just wanted to share a few things with you that we don't quite understand. Maybe you'll be able to shed some light on them."

"Of course, Detective. You can count on my full cooperation. I'll be able to sleep better once all this has been cleared up."

Since he had just stood to pick up the phone, Michael topped up his cup of freshly brewed free-trade organic coffee, grabbed his Moleskine and pen, and sat back down at his early-morning desk, attentive and ready to take notes. The detective spoke in an authoritative yet slightly hushed voice; Michael imagined him to be a workaholic, proud but beaten down by years of cold cases. Perhaps he was a veteran who had turned detective after a successful military career. Perhaps he had left the navy, haunted by his brothers in arms fallen in Kuwait, saddened by how the Department of Defense provided so little support to the grieving families of those American heroes. Unlikely, but perhaps. Michael imagined the man on the phone, his face somewhat weathered and angular, with an intense, piercing steel blue gaze. The first thing he wrote in his notebook was "Ed Harris."

"As you know, the emergency vehicles arrived right after the series of explosions, so we were able to pull the two bodies from the Jeep before they were completely charred. We thought we'd be able to get a few fingerprints off them, even just partials; but no, nothing. It was the same for dental impressions. Nothing. I mean the bodies had teeth, but we couldn't find a match in our databases. We did, however, have a small breakthrough this week when a new medical examiner specializing in severe burns came to do another autopsy. After careful examination, he was able to identify a feature both bodies had in common: a tattoo on the chest. According to our analysis, the tattoo consisted of two diagonal lines connecting the shoulders to the pubic bone, forming a sort of upside-down triangle. Also, judging by a region of one of the bodies that's still mostly intact, the lines seemed to be drawn in a particular pattern that could be a lightning bolt. Does that mean anything to you?"

"No, not really. Not that I can think of... I don't remember seeing anything like that before."

"Well, I figured I'd give it a shot. You never know. If you think of anything, call me back at this number. One more thing before I let you go: do you know if Ms. Couture ever lived in San Francisco? The kidnappers' car had San Francisco plates registered under a company name: Apollo Fitness. The gym's been closed for a few years now."

"Sorry, can't help you there either. I'll check with her and get back to you as soon as I can. Thanks for the update, Detective. It's very much appreciated."

Michael hung up the phone and sat chewing the end of his pen for a few minutes as he stared at the wall, deep in thought. He tried to focus on the clues but his mind fought him at every turn, hyperactive, rebellious, grasping fleetingly at everything that crossed it: lightning-bolt tattoos, exploding potassium permanganate, orange trees, the Honduras election, the Scott McKenzie song, "If You're Going to San Francisco," the Golden Gate Bridge, eating ice cream with his adoptive parents, lightning-bolt tattoos, "be sure to wear some flowers in your hair," Ed Harris, the article he'd read an hour ago on the grieving survivors of the Gulf War, lightning-bolt tattoos, an upside-down triangle, the hangar explosion scene at the end of *Bad Boys*, what he'd tell the press on the red carpet, "You're gonna meet some gentle people there," F-18 fighter planes, "*Peristasmoz!*", "*Peristasmoz!*" And on and on. From down the hall came the soft, sultry rhythm of Daphné's delicate footsteps as the hardwood floor creaked gently, already warm with April sunshine.

She was wearing an oversized pale-blue shirt that exposed her legs almost entirely, her hair a mess and her eyes half-asleep behind her glasses. She yawned as she moved through a home which, though it was not her own, had begun to feel more and more familiar. She headed to the kitchen, drawn by the aroma of fresh coffee, citrus, butter, and raisin toast.

You're rubbing off on me," she said. "I dreamt I was studying in Paris in the thirties and even though I was white, I was helping Damas, Senghor, and Césaire find a printer for the first issue of *L'Étudiant noir*."

"Nothing beats waking up to the feeling that you've done your part in deconstructing a logic that legitimizes the devaluing of indigenous peoples based on a so-called inferiority inherent to their culture. Good morning, my love."

"I bet it's even better waking up knowing that in a few short hours, the history of arthouse cinema will have to be rewritten thanks to you."

Daphné kissed Michael tenderly, her eyes still half-closed but sparkling.

"Who was on the phone?"

"The Miami police."

She stiffened slightly. The coffee was suddenly no longer a *sine qua non* for total wakefulness.

"Did they figure it out?"

"Not yet. But they're making headway. They found some strange tattoos on the two bodies. The detective didn't mention the other men, so I guess they haven't been able to track them down yet. He wanted me to ask you something, though. Did you ever live in San Francisco? Or do you have any connection to the city?"

"San Francisco? I don't think so... I was there for a conference a couple years ago, but after three days of hiding out in my hotel room to avoid all the pretentious cocktail banter I came back home. So I wouldn't have made much of an impression. That's the only time I've been. Why did they want to know?"

"The Jeep they took you in had San Francisco plates. The detective thought it might be a lead."

"Oh... If I think of anything, I'll let you know. Was that it?"

"That's it."

"Listen, let's not let all that get in the way of such an important day. We have a lot to do. I'm going to jump in the shower."

"You're right. We'll let the police do their job, and I'll concentrate on mine."

Daphné took a few steps toward the bathroom, slowed, then stopped.

"You know..."

She turned slowly toward Michael, hesitant yet seductive, fiddling with the shirt button between her breasts.

"... we could always make this day even more special."

"Daphné, we've discussed this."

"Okay, I know... Just thought it was worth a try."

Michael blew her a kiss, which she returned with a smile that barely concealed her humiliation. She

113

disappeared into the bathroom while Michael, his mind once again racing at a near-unbridled speed, sketched two lightning bolts in his notebook.

ON ASTROPOETICS

AS A PACKAGE OF DEHYDRATED SASHIMI orbited above him like a delicious satellite, Michael used his lunch break to touch up the final-sequence storyboards. This was the first time he'd painted in space, and he found the technical challenge quite stimulating. For optimal efficiency, he'd anchored his easel to the shuttle floor while he floated above it, curious to see the effects of weightlessness on the fluidity of his brush strokes. The painting he was working on was a cross between Kandinsky and Gauvreau, an abstract composition that wavered between mathematical precision and the visceral expression of a certain mystique. The colors were bright and balanced, never gaudy. Though the canvas was a modest size, Michael felt he was close to finally creating an image more expansive than nature, a fascinating yet frightening image, one beyond intellectualization, one that would force the viewer to confront their own limitations. In order to work, the final sequence in *Armageddon* needed to embody something unattainable for the human mind, to resist every possible variation of the horizon of expectations. Michael wanted to succeed where Kubrick's *2001* had failed.

"So this is your vision of the future, is it?" asked Neil deGrasse Tyson. The astrophysicist was a suave, mustachioed black man in his forties. He expressed himself with ease, and listened even more effortlessly.

"I feel as if abstraction is the only way to depict the future," answered Michael.

"Your humility is refreshing. But you're an artist; you've got imagination. Wouldn't you rather offer a clearer, representational vision of the future, one that would be of real use to you? Something people could get used to? It's often said that there are writers and filmmakers who have been able to predict the future through their work. Orwell, Verne, Huxley... I don't believe they predicted the future; I think they merely planted ideas that grew outside the confines of their stories. You know, to some extent, I'm jealous of you artists. Unlike mine, your cognition is not beholden to the laws and imperatives of the scientific method. You work outside of reality, while I'm confined within it. I try to decode the mysteries of the visible realm, but you have the greatest freedom of all: the freedom to create."

"You're making it sound as though I were the lucky one, as if my work were easy. I appreciate your enthusiasm, but you're mistaken, Professor. I too am trying to decode, to understand. I have no interest in a creative process that isn't rooted in something real. I actually think we have a lot in common: you're consumed by a need to explain the scientific mysteries of the universe, and I by a need to understand. We complete each other: my metaphysics is nothing without your physics."

"To understand—it's certainly a challenge, isn't it?" said Dr. Tyson. He smiled as he gazed out *Truth*'s window. "I quite enjoyed what you said during your speech just before takeoff. About the limits of the human mind. It's an interesting hypothesis. Defeatist, but interesting. After all, the question 'What is meaning?' is intrinsically linked to another: 'What is intelligence?' Certainly, one could argue that intelligence is the intersection of critical reasoning, knowledge, and curiosity. But in reality, how can we claim to understand when we consider our smallness within the universe? Right now, despite impressive technological advances, around 96% of the cosmos is beyond our understanding. We strut around with our laws and formulas that purport to explain the world with a few numbers and letters but, to tell you the truth, despite the great respect I have for Einstein, Newton, and Hawking, I find it difficult not to have doubts."

"Doubt. It's both my greatest ally and my worst enemy."

"Isn't it, though? Without doubt, we couldn't make progress... but how it slows that progress! For every moment of exaltation, there are hours of hesitation and anguish."

A furtive look of sadness flashed across Michael's face as he nodded in agreement.

"In the end," continued Dr. Tyson, "I draw little satisfaction from what humanity has accomplished to date. There's still so much to do, but all these advances that have changed how we interact with the world were also born out of questioning past knowledge. When I think that our ancestors considered this Earth, which you can see in all its splendor, the center of everything... Lucky for us, Copernicus first had the courage to doubt, to claim that our world was not that which, out of fear or conceit, we once thought it to be."

"You would say that, Professor. We should be giving Plato credit, not Copernicus. His rejection of the geocentric model is in fact nothing more than an astronomical transposition of the allegory of the cave."

Dr. Tyson opened his mouth to say something but changed his mind, giving Michael a humble smile instead. At the back of the cabin, Bruckheimer, who was pretending to do paperwork while in truth listening in on the conversation, was secretly pleased with his protégé's spirited remarks.

"You're probably right about Plato," continued Dr. Tyson eventually. "In fact, if I follow your logic, when we're faced with things we don't fully understand, like antimatter and black energy, in some ways we've got to admit that we're still chained to the back of that cave."

"I agree, but I also believe that the reason we find ourselves here, right now, on this shuttle, is because we're part of the few who try to look back over our shoulders and see what's going on around us. And unfortunately, as Plato also surmised, this search for Truth brings about a lot of disagreement, a lot of persecution from those who benefit the most from the illusory status quo. Tell me, Professor... May I ask you something?"

"Of course."

"How do your peers see you? What I mean is, do you feel respected and appreciated as you should be? Do people misunderstand or mistrust you? I often wonder if solitude is the price we pay for curiosity."

Dr. Tyson's signature smile faded. He looked around; his colleagues didn't seem to be paying him any attention, busy as they were collecting scientific data. To be safe, he moved in closer to Michael, lowered his voice, and confided, "Between you and me, yes, I do sometimes get the feeling the others are wary of me. It's because I've chosen the role of popularizer just as you have. What's the point of research if the findings can't be shared with the greatest number of people in a manner they can understand? Knowledge is a resource that should be accessible to all, not just to the elite; or rather, ignorance is a greater evil than the uprising it serves to suppress. I'm marginalized because I feel that raising awareness is more important than pure research, because I refuse to have my intellect serve only the interests of a league of astrophysicists. The general public values me, but my peers, whether out of jealousy or worry, seem to systematically minimize the importance of my discoveries. For instance, you were talking about Plato; my interest is Pluto. I've been studying this celestial body for years, and I recently arrived at the conclusion that, contrary to popular belief, Pluto is not a planet. At least not in the way Saturn, Mars, or Venus is, for example. It's actually a dwarf planet, a trans-Neptunian object like so many others. It's absurd to think of Pluto as one of the solar system's defining elements when there are so many objects in the same class that aren't! But don't think for a minute my discovery has been met with enthusiasm. Even the greatest scientific minds of our time want to maintain the established order! My campaign to rectify galactic factual errors is a losing battle. My arguments may be solid, but they've fallen on deaf ears; I'm told to go back to clowning around on TV. It's unfair. It's absurd. But I keep going, just as you do. I continue to believe my work is valid and necessary. And when I get tired or feel like throwing in the towel, do you know what I do? I watch one of your movies and it cheers me right up, because I know I'm not alone in my efforts to educate the public."

Michael's jaw dropped and his eyes widened. Dr. Tyson, while taller than the average male, was not a particularly large man; nonetheless, Michael felt pulled toward him, as though the astrophysicist possessed his very own gravitational field. He wanted to take Tyson in his arms and thank him for believing in him. He held back, however, opting for professionalism over emotion. Some light turbulence shook the shuttle. "So you're saying," said Michael, tearing up, "that you don't think I make trashy teen movies?"

"Ha! Are you kidding? If I thought that, I'd never have agreed to come on this mission! *Bad Boys* is definitely the best movie on decolonization since *The Battle of Algiers*! And *The Rock*... It's hard to think of another film that does such a brilliant job of paying tribute to academic knowledge and the wisdom of the Ancients! Not to mention its moving examination of isolation and misunderstanding. Honestly, few movies resonate with me like yours. Ignore the critics: in my eyes, you're already one of the greats."

Michael suddenly felt very light, but it had nothing to do with the weightlessness of space.

"And what's more," continued Dr. Tyson, "beyond the role of popularizer, what I find most interesting about your films is all the explosions. I see them as not just pyrotechnics but as a reflection on creation itself. In fact, I feel it's an obsession that we share. In my field, everything comes back to the original explosion, in both senses of the word 'original': the big bang. Without it, nothing would exist as we know it. Some attribute the world's creation to divine will, but we both know that's mere superstition, a fictional story for those with no imagination—or too much of one! Let's put it this way: if God exists, God is an explosion. In that sense, your movies reflect more than awe-inspiring intellectual rigor; I find they hold a certain mystique. I see your work as a metonymy for the universe, and it fascinates me."

"You're too generous, Professor. I appreciate your kind words, but you're giving me too much credit.

Really, my ambitions don't go as far as that. But thank you.... I, uh... Yeah, thanks..."

Michael had received so few compliments on his work in recent years that he'd forgotten how to react. In fact, while he would normally have accepted the words graciously, Michael gave an involuntary, slightly skeptical frown. Had the astrophysicist been truly honest with him, or was he messing with Michael in some elegant show of sadism? Such enthusiasm was suspicious. At the same time, Dr. Tyson's speech had seemed heart-felt.

"Well, I've taken up enough of your time. I'll leave you to your painting. I don't want to get in the way of art in the making. I should get back to work myself. But remember, my friend, you're not alone."

Dr. Tyson gave him a friendly wink, then went off to join his colleagues at the back of the cabin. Without quite knowing why, Michael saluted him, then tried to get back to finishing his storyboard, without much luck. Dr. Tyson's comments had rattled him. He digested them slowly, seriously, and his mistrust gradually gave way to a kind of excitement. "Of course," he murmured, as he gazed at his unfinished painting, "Yes..." The colors and lines on the canvas seemed to come to life with the exhilaration of this revelation: he no longer saw it as a simple impressionist sketch of future plans, but as a nebula, or rather, a supernova. He knew the explosion to be at the heart of his poetic art, but Dr. Tyson's perspective on the theme's meaning was something new.

For Michael, the explosion was about searching for his identity. It was the key to unlocking the enigma of his origins. He had always felt the necessity to blow things up was inherently selfish; never had he considered his obsession's relation to the universe. And while he'd chosen film as his main means of expression, he had always considered himself more of a philosopher than an artist. Maybe the mystery of meaning was in fact related to creation, rather than to reflection or analysis. What better way to understand the mechanisms obscuring the problem than to put oneself in the shoes of its architect? Perhaps the time had come to fully embrace his role as creator, to break free from the constraints of realism and plausibility, to resolve his concerns. This now struck him as a natural shift. After all, as Dr. Tyson had emphasized, the explosion is the first form of creation; it is above all invention rather than destruction. It is the light that denies the darkness. Michael was overcome with increasing elation. "Actually," he thought, "Tyson is wrong about one thing. If God exists, God is not an explosion. God is the force behind the explosion. Does that mean... When I create... Am I God? If—"

"Your attention please," interrupted the shuttle pilot. "We're approaching the comet tail. Please return to your seats and buckle your seatbelts. Things are going to get a little bumpy. Remember your training. This is what we prepared for."

Michael was shaken from his reverie. Feeling disoriented, he grabbed his canvas and headed toward his seat near the command station. The shuttle suddenly began to shudder. It was to be expected, but worrisome nonetheless. Out the window on his right, he could see *Independence* flying through a growing field of debris. Firmly planted on the chair marked DIRECTOR, he grabbed the strap with his free hand and braced himself. He closed his eyes, exhaled slowly, and whispered to himself calmly, "It's going to be okay."

Truth's windshield exploded into a puzzle of seemingly incompatible fragments.

ON HOLLYWOOD REPORTERS

THE ENGINE OF THE CONVERTED PORSCHE 911 Turbo limousine roared as a stream of flashes lit up Hollywood Boulevard like a brand-new shiny assault rifle. Sitting inside just moments before the valet opened the car door, Michael ran his thumb lovingly but nervously across Daphné's hand, mentally going over his answers for the press. He had never been to a premiere, not as big as this one at least. They'd obviously ask him to describe his process. To justify the film's tone as per the critical discourse running through it. Mary Hart, who he knew from Wesleyan, might ask him to clarify a few theoretical points, maybe provide a summary of *Dépossession du monde* to jog the memories of *Entertainment Tonight* viewers. He was well prepared for all that. But what if a reporter with a Lacanian bent asked him about his relationship with his mother? Or if they grilled him— you never know!—on his stance on neopragmatism? He wasn't really sure where he stood on the subject; while he was somewhat sympathetic to epistemic objectivity, he didn't want to come out publicly against Richard Rorty and damage their long-standing correspondence. The prospect of such questions left him momentarily breathless, as though an underwater explosion had gone off in his chest. His thumb strokes grew faster and Daphné, who was also nervous (though in her case, about seeing Simpson and Bruckheimer again), was pulled from her pensiveness by the increase in pressure.

"Michael? Pumpkin? Are you OK?"

Michael turned abruptly to Daphné, caught red-handed in a fit of anguish. He smiled, then sighed, relieved she was there.

"You're so beautiful. You take my breath away."

Michael and Daphné exchanged a reassuring look, kissed, then, brought back to reality by a sudden clamor, stepped out through the door that was being held open for them. The red carpet was packed on both sides. The collective cheers faded when the director stepped out instead of Will Smith, but seeing how dashing he looked in his tux, with his beautiful mane of hair, the crowd began screaming his name too. Michael waved to the sea of faces and took Daphné by the waist. Mary Hart walked over to him, mic lowered.

"Michael Bay," she said, smiling.

"Mary Hart," he replied, all set for their conversation.

"Not surprised to see you here, Michael. You were made for the red carpet! You were already a glowing example of discipline and flair at Wesleyan; you've always been an inspiration to me."

Michael flashed an idiotic smile and bashfully lowered his gaze. Behind him, Daphné frowned.

"That's so kind... And congratulations to you as well on your work. On-air reviews would be a thing of the past without it. Your perspective helps keep our arts scene going."

"Oh stop, Michael. That's a bit of a stretch. But I appreciate the compliment. Can I interview you for *ET*?"

"It would be a pleasure, Mary. Do you want to talk about *Dépossession*? It's true that Jacques Berque isn't as well known as Césaire or Fanon, but his metadiscourse is still key to my arguments. I can condense them into a couple minutes."

"Sure, maybe. We'll see where the conversation takes us... Ready?"

"When you are."

Mary Hart signaled to her cameraman, who started rolling, and picked up the mic.

"This is Mary Hart, here with Michael Bay, the young director of the new movie *Bad Boys*. Tell us, Michael, who are you wearing tonight?"

"Who am I wearing? Sorry?"

"Your tux, Michael. Who's the designer?"

"The designer? I'm not really sure... Hugo Boss? Versace? One of those two..."

"And tell us, Michael, who's with you tonight?"

Michael cleared his throat, hesitating.

"This is Daphné."

The camera's light momentarily blinded Daphné, who, much to her discomfort, was suddenly the focus of attention.

"Tell us, Daphné, you've chosen a dress that completely covers your back instead of the backless look that's all the rage right now—how come? It's a gutsy choice!"

"Backless? All the rage? I... I'm not really sure... I wore it because it's my favorite dress."

"And why the glasses?"

"My glasses? So I can see...? I...?"

"Viewers at home, call the number on the bottom of your screen to let *Entertainment Tonight* know what you think: Daphné Bay's glasses, hot or not? The answer tomorrow! *Bad Boys*, starring Will Smith and Martin Lawrence, in theaters April 7th. Back to you, Bob."

The camera went dark.

"Thanks, you two. That's all the time I've got. Good luck with the movie!"

Mary Hart turned and made her way through the crowd to Téa Leoni, who had just arrived on the red carpet in a backless dress. Michael and Daphné stood there, confused, their offended silence a counterpoint to the cacophony around them.

"Wow, such an in-depth interview," said Daphné bitterly.

"I don't understand. She seemed so brilliant in college, so I assumed... Have you ever seen *Entertainment Tonight*? Is that the kind of journalism they do?"

"They're rapacious frauds, not journalists. The only thing they care about is glitter and gossip."

"I'm sorry I subjected you to that..."

There was a brief silence. Daphné exhaled through her nose. "It's OK. This is *your* night. Forget it. Chin up and smile, pumpkin. No matter what happens tonight, you know I'll always be proud of you."

Michael smiled, overwhelmed with love. He kissed Daphné on the red carpet.

From the outside, the Chinese Theater looked more suited to dinner than a movie. The smell of collagen hung in the air. Full of renewed confidence, Michael wanted to immerse himself in the moment and etch into his very being the tiniest details of that night, which he felt sure was the start of something big. The first thing he noticed was how the people seemed carefully arranged on the red carpet, methodically stratified like one of those topographic maps of the San Fernando Valley he'd studied with his traitorous father; only now he was the highest point of elevation. Around him the crowd was gathered in winding, concentric shapes made up of the following layers: the stars at the summit—a category to which, it would seem, he now belonged—then, as you got closer to sea level, the public relations people, journalists, photographers, elegantly dressed security officers, fans, and the rest. At the edge of the crowd, the producers were talking amongst themselves. The noise nearly drowned out the sound of helicopters flying gracefully overhead, backlit by an orange sunset. The warm, late-afternoon colors coordinated perfectly with the enormous movie poster on a nearby wall featuring a wide shot of Martin Lawrence, Téa Leoni, and Will Smith staring aggressively into the camera, both men with guns pointed, a Porsche in the background. "Whatcha Gonna Do?" it asked. "Whatcha gonna do to restore power to your subjugated people?" was the obvious subtext. It was beautiful. Michael turned in a slow circle, eyes bright, soaking in the whole of this event in his honor. Opposite the movie poster hung another image, adding a spectacular, dramatic feel to the first. It was a poster for Don Simpson/Jerry Bruckheimer Films. A vast stormy sky. Two giant bolts of lightning converging.

Michael froze, then felt someone come up from behind and tousle his hair with a firm yet gentle hand. It was Bruckheimer. "Tonight's the night! It's time to show the world that your intellect, your understanding of Truth, is ready for eternal recognition."

"*Peristasmoz*," replied Michael, defiantly.

"Excuse me?"

"*Peristasmoz*. Do you know what that means?"

"I couldn't say, Michael. What language is that?"

"You see, I thought you might be able to clear that up for me. Or maybe Mr. Simpson. You remember Daphné, don't you? You know, from that wonderful night in Miami at Flavor Nightclub in Coconut Grove."

"Yes, of course I remember the young lady. I'm happy to see you're safe and sound after that unfortunate

130

misadventure," said Bruckheimer, avoiding Daphné's eye.

"Where is Mr. Simpson?"

"He's trying to reason with the executives. It's all part of the job."

"I'd like to ask him about a certain phone call placed minutes before Daphné's abduction. My rational mind tends to find coincidences all too suspicious."

"What are you saying, son? That Mr. Simpson had something to do with that sinister incident? Please, listen to yourself! You're clearly confused."

"Am I? Tell me, Mr. Bruckheimer, what does your production company logo represent?"

Bruckheimer pursed his lips slightly and swallowed slowly. The crowd around them was paying no attention to their conversation. "Where are you going with this, Michael? I find your tone inappropriate. Don't forget who you're speaking to."

"I got a call this morning. It was Detective Hummel from the Miami PD. He's in charge of Daphné's kidnapping case."

"And...?"

"Why did one of the assailants have your logo tattooed on his chest?"

"I have no idea. Maybe he's a fan?"

"This isn't a joke!" said Michael, raising his voice.

"Calm down!" said Bruckheimer brusquely. "You're tenacious, Michael. I'll give you that. But you're insolent, and you're ignorant. In fact you're doubly ignorant: you think you understand, but you know nothing."

A voice came from the loudspeakers: *All guests please make your way to the main theater. The screening will begin shortly.*

"Free your mind of what you cannot understand. Enjoy your evening. You're about to honor the memory of the victims of colonialism with a powerful, nuanced debut and claim your spot in the history of ideas. Tonight marks the start of a great career. So please, don't let yourself get distracted," Bruckheimer added, finally glancing in Daphné's direction, then walking off.

"I knew it. They hate me."

"Do you think I'm crazy to think they had something to do with the kidnapping? Look at how Bruckheimer treats you! And Simpson calling God knows who just before you were taken... But most of all the lightning bolts, the tattoos... Oh Daphné, I don't know what to think! Maybe I'm overanalyzing things."

"Let's go sit down. We'll leave right after the film. I don't like it here."

Hours later, when the many event photographers would go on to develop their negatives of the evening, they'd have a field day with the two long faces, contrasting as they did with the seasoned smiles of the other guests. And as Michael grappled with the hazards of overanalyzing, the paparazzi would lap up his expression. The mercenaries would jump at the chance to provide the newspapers and magazines they worked for with fodder for morning headlines like "The Bays: A Marriage on the Brink of Explosion!" "Michael Bay and Téa Leoni: Michael Confesses All to Wife!" "Michael Bay Comes Out: His Wife in Shock!" and "Another Creepy Hollywood Director?" Cashing in on the entirely fabricated distress of a couple they had zero concern for, the shutter-happy photographers would congratulate themselves on their perfect shots as they spent their spoils on cocaine and fellatio. But for now, Michael and Daphné, powerless against the cynical lens of Hollywood's reporters, entered the kitsch oriental-style building and sat down in the seats reserved for them, Michael's heart racing as the lights dimmed for the first screening of *Bad Boys*.

ON THE GRAPES OF CORINTH

DAPHNÉ CAREFULLY STEPPED FORWARD holding a lantern, searching for Michael in the overgrown woods near the tent. The sun was still shining, but only a few rays made it through the thick, filter-like foliage, lending a greenish glow to the scene. A hypothetical woodpecker could be heard now and then, as could other birds cooing to each other, making for a repetitive yet sporadic late-afternoon soundtrack. The campsites adjacent were empty, so Michael had plenty of space to locate the perfect hiding spot and reflect on the meaning of dissimulation. Daphné's clothes smelled of campfire. Behind her, the rustle of leaves in the underbrush made her jump; she whirled around with a victorious "Ah-ha!" only to find, to her dismay, that she'd been fooled by the nervous scampering of an eastern chipmunk. She noted, with some anxiety as to her professional future, that despite her vast experience in libraries, she was ill-equipped for this type of search.

About fifty feet away, Michael had become one with a mountain laurel, like a Navy SEAL waiting in ambush.

He breathed in time with the breeze. Face covered in mud, belly to the ground, he carefully, fondly observed his lover's movements. The last few months had been so pleasant, so full of tender smiles, kisses, embraces, winks, lengthy discussions, comforting words, discoveries, kindness, and uncontrollable laughter, that he'd let himself forget, if only briefly, the bitterness about his origins that had filled him since childhood. Perhaps most of all, these moments had proven to him that his heart was not beyond repair, that he was still capable, despite his bruised trust, of losing himself in another. In her. No disrespect to his producers—the misogyny they were often accused of was beginning to seem less and less a mere aesthetic choice. She was so beautiful with her messy ponytail, fleece jacket, hiking boots, and dirty jeans. So authentic.

"Michael? Pumpkin? Where are you? I give up. You win! I can't find you... Come out! Let's go down to the water before it gets dark."

The Corinth campground was situated on the banks of the Hudson River in Saratoga County, between Highway 87 and the Adirondack Park. They'd set off in Michael's old Dodge Ram as soon as he'd finished shooting *Bad Boys*, anxious to get some time alone. Daphné had never quite gotten used to the excessive LA lifestyle and wanted to escape California and its superfluities for a while. As an undergraduate student in Connecticut, she had often driven Highway 87, passing all those picturesque little towns, on her way to visit her parents. So she had suggested to Michael that, to strengthen the bond between them, they take the road north, stopping in at the towns they found most inspiring to camp out in nature, far from wealth, artifice, and social niceties. Stripped bare of these obligations, away from everything, they would find out if their love lived up to its promise.

"Michael? I've been looking for you for an hour. I'm done. Wonderful as you are, you're trying my patience. If you don't come out this minute I'm going on ahead by myself."

Her ultimatum delivered, she waited a few seconds more, listening carefully, convinced she'd get results. If you'd asked her just then whether her threat was out of irritation or simply a playful ploy, she might have hesitated to say. No doubt she was testing the parameters within which their relationship was set to grow. She was sorry she'd raised her voice, but the lack of movement in the leaves around her confirmed she hadn't taken things too far. "Well I hope you're enjoying yourself! I'll be by the river if you're looking for me!" said Daphné with a dramatic sigh. She turned around to find Michael waiting at the picnic table with a beach bag containing a bunch of grapes, sunscreen, two American flag towels, various novels and volumes of critical theory, and a ball and two baseball gloves. His complexion seemed smoother than ever as she gazed at his face.

"Ready?" he said to Daphné, who was surprised but delighted.

136

They took a narrow path to the river through a clearing where magnificent butterflies flitted between enormous flowers. The air was pleasant and fresh. Hand in hand, they walked silently, smiling, each second confirming all they'd hoped to confirm. Although the riverbank inspired nature interpretation more than relaxation, they began to unwind as they were hit with the intoxicating impression of being completely cut off from the world. In the full sun, the usual March chill no longer precluded nudity and so, while Michael was busy reading a sign explaining the robin's mating cycle, Daphné began disrobing behind him.

"I'm sorry I raised my voice just then. Please don't think I was angry. I guess I just missed you. It was torture knowing you were so close but that I couldn't reach you... I needed to feel you close to me. I just don't want you to think I'm trying to be controlling. Um... Could you help me with my sunscreen, Michael?"

Michael turned and found Daphné leaning back on her towel, slowly bringing a grape to her lips, naked except for her black lace underwear. There was something cat-like and defiant in her eyes. She chewed the grape slowly, almost gracefully, then with both hands on the ground behind her, she subtly arched her back as though offering up her neck. The most prolific romance novelist would have struggled to describe the sheer perfection of her breasts, while the fullness of her curves would have inspired even the most unimaginative of car designers. Her body was as gorgeous as the Victoria's

Secret models Michael had often worked with; indeed it even surpassed theirs, her beauty more poetic than plastic. The breeze came in off the river to gently caress her skin, turning each and every pore into a goose-bump. She shivered. Realizing it was a show meant for him, Michael played spectator for a few seconds, then moved closer, sidestepping the towel to come kneel down behind her.

"Tilt your head forward so I can get your whole back."

Daphné obeyed, intrigued. Michael dug around in his bag, pulled out the tube of lotion, and squeezed some into his left palm. Daphné's breathing became syncopated as Michael, starting with her shoulders, began rubbing her back with his strong, capable hands. Daphné let out a few involuntary groans. Her head fell forward, moving sensually from left to right and right to left as though in unison with the movements of the coconut-scented massage. She felt the pressure move to her lower back, sending a flutter through her stomach.

"Did you know that robins are monogamous? Most couples are completely faithful right up until one of them dies."

After thoroughly rubbing Daphné's lower back, Michael's hands moved up either side, edging near but never touching the contours of her breasts, her nipples erect. He traced delicate circles with his fingers, making her head spin. Then moved down again, his powerful hands caressing her hips. The March air suddenly felt overwhelmingly hot.

"Alright, all done. You're good," said Michael, standing back up. "I think I'll get some sun and finish rereading *Sun Tzu*. What would you like—one of your thesis books? A novel maybe?"

Daphné lay there confused and dejected.

"What? I... Um... You're not done. You forgot my chest."

"Your chest? But you're perfectly capable of doing that by yourself! You're so cute... So what'll it be: theory or pleasure?"

"Pleasure. I thought that was obvious."

Michael knelt down by the bag, hesitated for a moment, then stood back up and handed his sweetheart a copy of *Hamletmachine*. On the ground, a few grapes had begun to wither.

"Can you move?" she said finally, more surprised than angry. "You're blocking my sun."

The forest was almost completely dark save a few smoking embers and a dome of light against which two shadows held each other in a complicit kiss.

"You're not too nervous about meeting my parents?"

"Should I be?"

"I don't know. I don't think so. Actually I'm the one who's nervous."

"I won't embarrass you. I promise. I'll try not to at least."

"I know you won't. That's not what I mean. Just promise me you won't be disappointed."

"Disappointed?"

"I'm the first person in my family to get a degree, you know. My father worked at a hardware store his whole life. My mother is a waitress with a side job cleaning rich people's houses in town. When I go back, I often feel as though the distance between us is expanding, as though it's harder and harder to talk to them, as though we live in two different worlds. It makes me sad. I love them so much. They're such good people, so devoted... To be honest I'm a bit scared that meeting them and talking with them will make you change your mind about me."

"Daphné, honey, look at me. I love you. I've never said that to anyone before. And I already know you're the only one I'll ever say it to. We have something special. Something indestructible. Trust me. You're an amazing woman, and I'm sure your parents are amazing, too."

"One other thing... they don't speak English very well."

"Then I'll get to practice my French."

Daphné smiled, reassured.

"How do you say it again? About the soup being good? *Cette soupe est câlisse bonne*?"

"Haha! No! First of all, it'd be pretty strange for you to swear the first time you meet my parents. I suppose it'd show your interest in the local culture, but still... It's like if I said 'fuck' the first time I met your parents. It'd

140

feel too weird... But if you really want to know, it's *Cette soupe est câlissement bonne*, or *Cette soupe est bonne en câlisse*, or even *C'est une câlisse de bonne soupe.* You can do a lot with *câlisse*. In those examples '*câlisse*' is an adverb, but you can also use it as a noun—I love you, *mon câlisse*—or as a verb—you can *câlisser une volée* to someone (knock their lights out)—or as a verb with a prefix—*décâlisser* something—or as an adjective or epithet—He seems *décâlissé*—or simply an interjection—*Câlisse*, this soup is good! or even *Câlisse!* Quit messing around and kiss me!"

Michael's eyes twinkled as he leaned in to kiss her.

"Thank you. You're a *câlisse de bonne* teacher."

"And you're a fast learner," she replied, blushing. "But if you really want to swear properly in French you'll need a few more lessons. It's an art. So, what about your parents? Will I get to meet them someday?"

Michael tensed imperceptibly and, feigning discomfort, shifted on the inflatable mattress.

"Do you think there's a leak? Maybe I should pump it up a bit."

"No, it's fine. I'm still comfortable."

Daphné left it at that and rolled onto her back. With clear skies in the forecast, they'd left the two mesh windows at the top of the tent open and outside they could see a sliver of starry sky through a small opening in the trees.

"You know, there's an observatory near my parents' place. We could stop in if we have time."

"That sounds nice. I've always loved the stars. Which is probably why I love your eyes so much."

"God, you're so *quétaine*..."

"*Quétaine*? What does that mean?"

"I'm not sure how to translate it. Like cheesy, or ridiculous even. Like you're trying too hard. But it's cute—I don't actually mind. I love you too, Michael. You're the best thing that's happened to me in a long time. I know it isn't good to talk about old boyfriends when you're in a new relationship, but I'll just say this: I've been let down a lot. I've often felt betrayed by men who I thought were serious, but who weren't completely truthful with me. I was just a way to pass the time. I've been hurt so many times that trust doesn't come easily now. But it's different with you. I feel stupid saying that, like I never learned from my mistakes. Except that there's something about you, Michael, that makes me feel as though nothing before this matters. Maybe it's how kind you are—a sort of purity you possess. And you're obviously brilliant. It makes me feel that I can trust you. That there's hope for a happy future."

Michael's vision grew blurry with emotion. He kissed Daphné again, but it was a sloppy kiss, possibly due to the fluids trickling down his face. They said goodnight, then snuggled up like a couple of spoons under the unzipped sleeping bag. Daphné pressed her backside against Michael's crotch, to no effect. She gave up after a few minutes and slid her hand between her thighs.

The next morning Daphné and Michael took down the tent, laughed about how hard it was to get all the pieces into the tiny zippered bag, made toast on the leftover embers from the evening before, dumped the dishwater onto the fire to be sure it was out, then, after Michael had discreetly checked he still had the engagement ring he'd bought just a few days earlier, they left Corinth for the town of Lac-Mégantic, Quebec.

ON SUFFERING

DAPHNÉ WAS QUIET. Over the past months, Michael had
learnt to respect the silence that inevitably followed
when they watched a movie together. The first time
he'd experienced her curious post-film trance was after
he'd introduced her to Tarkovsky, whose work she'd
not been familiar with despite her PhD-level studies
in film. Following a screening of *Stalker* at the local
arthouse theater, in a rush of excitement over the poetry
of the film, Michael had hastened to seek Daphné's
impressions. "So, what did you think? Isn't it absolutely
amazing? Have you ever seen such brilliant examples of
Deleuzian pure optical and sound situations?" Daphné
had stood up, slowly putting on her jacket, but had not
paid him any attention. Frowning, she had exited the
theater, Michael in tow as he sought some element of
interest to rouse her from this stasis. As Deleuze hadn't
worked, he tried Pasolini. "It's total *Cinema di poesia*,
don't you think? A reflection on cinema's potential to
go beyond simple narrative and achieve expressiveness

144

where image-signs possess all the purity and subjectivity of language signs. Tarkovsky illustrates it to a T, doesn't he? Daphné?" She was in her own world, imperturbable. Michael had started to get nervous: had he done something wrong? Had he unknowingly reopened an old wound? Had she found the Zone's inherent plurisemy disturbing? Was she upset with him? Why wasn't she answering him? Was this it? The end of their burgeoning love? They had been walking in the crisp Santa Barbara night for ten minutes. Michael, perplexed yet resigned, fell silent too, adding to his malaise but at least delaying the parting of ways he felt was inevitably at hand.

"It was really good," she finally concluded, casually.

"So... You liked it?" said Michael, relieved but slightly wary.

"Yes, I really did. It was magnificent—a truly dream-like work inspired by a framework of free indirect discourse that creates the subjectivity needed to poeticize the image-sign. It's going to be a huge film. Thanks for taking me to see it, pumpkin!"

"I really thought you hated it and were upset with me..."

"Upset?!! Pumpkin! Anything but! I'm so, so thankful!"

"But you were quiet for so long..."

"Don't take it personally, sweetie. It's just that, well... I believe film is an inherently individual experience. What I mean is, I like watching movies with other people, and I know I'll especially enjoy the ones I see with you, but movies trigger an almost biological or chemical reaction inside me. My brain goes haywire trying to process the signs flooding my hermeneutic understanding... So when the movie is over, I'm still in the midst of analyzing and organizing, debating the ideas internally, before I come to a conclusion. It's something I can't control."

Michael had given Daphné an infinitely tender smile. So as they walked toward the hall of the Chinese Theater amid the crowd's applause, Michael did not think anything of Daphné's silence. He was in fact particularly respectful of it. He cherished it.

It had been thirty minutes since the credits of *Bad Boys* had rolled to the music of Inner Circle. Daphné found a spot at the back of room, avoiding eye contact with the crowd. Michael kept an eye on her as he discussed phenomenology with Will Smith, Martin Lawrence, and Nic Cage. Time passed. The pride of seeing his work so meticulously analyzed by the woman he loved was slowly turning to discomfort. Almost an hour after the cocktail event started, Daphné finally turned to look at him. He took the cue, excused himself from the group, and joined her away from the crowd, ready for the verdict.

"So?" he started off the conversation, smiling and feigning an expression of fear.

Daphné slowly opened her mouth to answer, but changed her mind and looked away.

"Darling?" Michael tried again.

146

She waited a moment before replying.

"*Câlisse*! You've got to be kidding me!" she said finally, eyes wild. "That was your film on decolonization? THAT was your goddamn film on Césaire? Give me a fucking break. That was just another shitty teenage action flick! You're telling me that I've just spent the last four months of my life thinking I was dating a genius, and it turns out you're just another director who makes shitty blockbusters? Perfect—this is just fucking perfect! It did seem weird to me that anyone with the slightest bit of intelligence would decide to work with Jerry Bruckheimer! Jerry Fucking Bruckheimer! It's not like the guy produced *Germania anno zero* or *Citizen Kane*. His biggest achievement is *Top Gun*! Fucking *Top Gun*! Fighter jets and poorly disguised homoeroticism. *Câlisse*.... I just don't get you... I mean, if you were trying to make me think you were so brilliant just to get in my pants, that'd make you an asshole, but at least you'd have been able to get something out of your goddamn masquerade. But no, no sex for you! Because Mr. Bay wants to live 'the most poetic and powerful of loves.' God! I've got news for you: being an atheist and a virgin at 30 is not something to be proud of. It means you're a fucking loser! You know what? Sleeping with you probably would have been like sleeping with a teenager anyway. Because let me tell you something else: it's fucking weird that you don't have a single hair on your body. I guess that's why you need to pump so much testosterone into your movies, to compensate for the fact

147

that you have none! You're not a man, Michael. *Câlisse!* You're a deranged prepubescent asshole! And I'm an idiot. I could have spent the last four months writing my thesis instead of giving in to the weird whims of a sociopath. What am I going to tell my thesis advisor? Fuck! You can take your goddamn trigger-happy movie, shove it up your ass, and try to forget we ever met. Fuck you, Michael Bay."

Daphné stormed off, leaving Michael completely stunned for the second time that evening. There it was. She'd left him. He'd been abandoned again. His ears rang as though a bomb had gone off nearby. He didn't know who to turn to. He was alone.

Michael felt someone come from behind and tousle his hair with a familiar firm, tender hand.

"She's not one of us, Michael," said Bruckheimer. "She can't understand."

Michael didn't answer. He didn't dare put his trust back in the producer so easily, now that he had his suspicions.

"Distraction," said Bruckheimer. "*Perispasmós*, if that's what you were trying to tell me earlier, means more or less 'distraction.' It's Greek."

Michael gave him a look full of uncertainty.

"I had nothing to do with Daphné's kidnapping. I'll say it again, but I can't force you to believe me."

Michael let out a long sigh. Finally, he said, "Do you honestly think I screwed up? That the homage to Césaire doesn't come across at all? That *Bad Boys* is really just a crappy teen flick?"

"No," replied Bruckheimer, stroking his protégé's cheek, "on the contrary. *Bad Boys* is a glorious success. History will prove it. That woman simply doesn't have the necessary sensibility. We felt it from the start."

"But if such an intelligent woman can't understand my art, then who will?"

"I understand you. And others will too. Your process is brilliant yet opaque. Not everyone can be a brilliant mind."

"I don't want to go home. I'll only feel her absence."

"Then stay here with us. Wherever I am, you're always welcome."

"I'd rather get out of here. To forget what just happened. I think I've earned a break."

"You're right. Let's go to my place. You can stay a few days and clear your head. We can leave right now if you'd like."

Michael threw his arms gratefully around Bruckheimer, whose warm, gentle embrace almost fully enveloped the younger man, their bodies pressing against one another. Michael felt safe. He felt loved.

Arm in arm, the two men left the Chinese Theater, Bruckheimer humming *Take My Breath Away* into Michael's ear.

"PROBABLY PSYCHOTROPIC DEMENTIA," said the first assistant director, rolling his eyes.

The shooting schedule for *The Rock* had been delayed yet again due to Sean Connery's antics, his mind and body in the throes of a recreational hit of acid. In the backlot near the buffet, the Scot was stirring up another commotion: dressed in the costume he had worn for the movie *Zardoz*—essentially a pair of red briefs held up by suspenders crisscrossed over his hairy chest—he was engaged in an absurd and entirely ineffective attack on the production employees, who were trying to reason with him. His expression shifted from confusion to fear to bliss to anger to idiocy as he bellowed utterances it seemed only an exorcist could decipher. Connery waved his empty hands in the air as though wielding invisible nunchuks. Then he froze and stared wide-eyed into space. The dolly operators and other production assistants now surrounding him stopped as well, hesitant, as though waiting for a surprise attack. Connery knelt down, hands clasped together like a choirboy, and began muttering, apparently in some sort of spiritual trance. The technicians crept closer, ready to overpower him. When one finally made a move, Connery jumped to his feet at near-superhuman speed, let out a deafening shriek, and took off laughing. Then he was gone.

"I don't think we'll be able to shoot his scenes today," said the second assistant director.

"It was a bad idea from the start," said Michael. "Sean Connery... I don't know what Bruckheimer and Simpson were thinking."

"We'll have to move today's schedule around. Any ideas?"

"The studio still isn't happy with the screenplay. I know there are two screenwriters working on a rewrite for some of the sections right now. I should go check in, keep an eye on everything. You take a break. Actually, no: go read this." Michael took Sun Tzu's *Art of War* out of his shoulder bag and handed it to his assistant.

He walked over to the trailer where the two young screenwriters were working. Relations with the production company had soured, and Disney had hired the pair, concerned that Michael and his colleagues were intent on "corrupting young minds." Michael didn't really understand. He was nervous.

He'd had better days.

His face was drawn and he'd lost a bit of his spark. The events of the past weeks had been a drain on his morale. Sure, the box office success of *Bad Boys* had

151

allowed him to embark straight away on a second and more personal feature film, *The Rock*. But though he was determined, just as the Lumières philosophers had been, to have his work widely circulated and thus contribute to developing the critical eye of the masses, Michael could not shake a painful sense of failure. He'd been rejected by the woman he loved, the woman he'd most wanted to impress. And he'd been rejected by the academic critics, whom he knew were key to real historical recognition. Not a single peer-reviewed journal had made the slightest mention of him; only publications read by the general public—essentially promotional materials and grocery-aisle publications—had taken an interest in his first film. Reaction to his film-essay had been summed up in a few keywords that could be applied to almost anything: "exciting," "frenetic," "hilarious," "breathtaking," and the like. Not a single critic had brought up, even in passing, the examination of the emancipation of black Americans. The institution he so respected, to which he had given so much during his years of learning, and from which he expected recognition above all, had abandoned him. More than ever, Michael understood the rage of soldiers whose brothers had fallen in combat and into oblivion.

The distant sound of the weapons specialist firing blanks rang out as Michael stepped into the trailer the screenwriters were using as an office. Inside it smelled of weed and cheeseburgers. The two men, their faces barely visible through the thick smoke, paid little attention to the intrusion, engrossed as they were in frenetic conversation. Several pairs of women's shoes were strewn haphazardly across the floor, though there were no women in sight. Before speaking up, Michael paused to listen.

"Kelly McGillis," one of the writers was arguing, "she's heterosexuality. She's saying: no, no, no, no, no, no, go the normal way, play by the rules, go the normal way. They're saying no, go the gay way, be the gay way, go for the gay way, all right? That is what's going on throughout that whole movie... He goes to her house, right? It looks like they're going to have sex, you know, they're just kind of sitting back, he's takin' a shower and everything. They don't have sex. He gets on the motorcycle, drives away. She's like, 'What the fuck, what the fuck is going on here?' Next scene, next scene you see her, she's in the elevator, she is dressed like a guy. She's got the cap on, she's got the aviator glasses, she's wearing the same jacket that the Iceman wears. She is, okay, this is how I gotta get this guy, this guy's going toward the gay way, I gotta bring him back, I gotta bring him back from the gay way, so I'm gonna do that through subterfuge, I'm gonna dress like a man. All right? That is how she approaches it. All right, but the REAL ending of the movie is when they fight the MiGs at the end, all right? Because he has passed over into the gay way. They are this gay fighting fucking force, all right? And they're beating the Russians, the gays are beating the Russians. And it's over, and they fucking land, and Iceman's been

153

trying to get Maverick the entire time, and finally, he's got him, all right? And what is the last fucking line that they have together? They're all hugging and kissing and happy with each other, and Ice comes up to Maverick, and he says, 'Man, you can ride my tail, anytime!' And what does Maverick say? 'You can ride mine!'"

"Hahaha! You're such an asshole," responded the second writer. "That's a total crock. It's just some paranoid overanalysis by a right-wing nut who thinks everything is liberal propaganda."

"I'm not dissing it, all's I'm saying is it's subversive genius! It's subversion on a massive level! *Top Gun* is one of the greatest fucking Hollywood screenplays ever written!"

"Um," said Michael, finally cutting in, "I think you're bending the truth a bit for the sake of your analysis, which is, let's just say, reaching. The line is actually: 'You can be my wingman anytime.' But I admit it's an entertaining theory despite the somewhat flawed methodology—the kind of thing that's perfect for a fictional work... say Rory Kelly's *Sleep With Me*..."

The writers swatted away the smoke to get a better look at who was talking, giving Michael the chance to confirm his hypothesis as to their identities as well. "Mr. Tarantino, Mr. Sorkin, pleased to have you on my set. Disney has clearly got two talented writers on the case. A Palme d'Or winner and an expert on military drama. I'm relieved! Can I join you?"

"Sure, why not?" replied Tarantino. "You wanna burger? We've got a dozen left."

"Thanks, but no, I'm allergic to sesame," said Michael, feeling for the Epipen he kept on him at all times. So... any progress?"

"Yes, I think we're finally getting somewhere," said Sorkin. "We don't have much to work with though, I have to say. I don't find it very believable."

Michael's smile dissolved, but he forced himself to remain professional.

"What isn't believable, in your opinion?"

"A bunch of stuff," continued Sorkin.

"For one thing, when the Marines infiltrate Alcatraz from below, led by Mason. They trust this old guy because he's managed to escape before. That, I like. But when they get to the part with the furnace, that's just stupid. Mason knows exactly when the machine fires up, so he goes first and rolls through the small passage underneath the furnace. Then, once he's on the other side, he opens the door so Goodspeed and the soldiers can go through to the next room. Okay, I get that it's supposed to spectacular, but what I'm wondering is, why the hell did Mason bother memorizing the timing of the furnace mechanism if all he had to do in the end, I mean when he was escaping, was open a door?"

"A fucking door!" added Tarantino.

"It's rhetoric," Michael explained. "With his demonstration of coolheadedness and familiarity with the premises, Mason establishes his superiority over the others. He refutes their smug self-importance and forces them to respect him. Is there a more definitive argument

155

than risking one's life for no reason just to prove a point? Not even Schopenhauer went that far!"

"Okay... no, I'm not convinced," said Tarantino. "It would work better if he swore more or went off on an epic rant about Hot Rods or his favorite Beatles albums."

"Or a long speech about how evil the media is and how they're really just conditioning us to mindlessly give in to the whims of big corporations," suggested Sorkin.

"You know," said Michael, "I'm not sure your suggestions really capture the spirit of the film..."

"That's another thing: what exactly *is* the spirit of the film? What are you trying to say? We're not sure we really get it."

"Essentially, I'm trying to show that we can solve the world's problems through academic knowledge and the wisdom of the Ancients."

The two writers furrowed their brows disapprovingly.

"Why try to find a solution to the world's problems," Tarantino argued, "when they're the reason we get to express ourselves as creators of discourse?"

"Our entire art depends on conflict," added Sorkin. "Conflict is the spark for our inspiration. The tirades we're known for? They all stem from disagreement. How can we contribute to a film that's trying to resolve them—even if only symbolically? No, that would be seriously counter-productive. We're here to do one thing and one thing only: convince the audience. That's why they hired us."

"It's the audience's job to ask the questions, not be convinced of anything. The takeaway has to come from within, from a slow reflection, not from some smooth-talker's hypnosis," said Michael.

"There's no greater power than persuasion."

"And there's no more powerful tool than doubt. What exactly do you want to convince the public of, anyway?"

"Everything, nothing—it doesn't matter. As long as we draw them in and gain their sympathy. As long as they come away thinking we're brilliant."

"You're mercenaries of the mind. You have no use for the Truth."

"And you," said Sorkin, raising his voice, "you can't handle the Truth!"

Michael, his mind reeling from Sorkin's intellectual shortcut, wanted to explode into a powerful stream of rebuttals. He held himself back, irritated but diplomatic.

"Your discourse is vapid," he said after a pause. "All you want is to get a reaction."

"And you and your friends," replied Sorkin, "all you want is to corrupt the youth of this great country. You're a threat to the established order—the natural order of things. It's our job to protect that order, to tell people what they need to hear and know, such as, for example, that an attack could come at any time."

Michael felt powerless in the face of a world view so diametrically opposed to his own. He got up to leave.

"Don't wreck my film," said Michael, as he opened the door.

"We don't give a shit about your fucking movie!" yelled Tarantino, his cry muffled by yet another mouthful of cheeseburger.

The brilliant sun shining over the set couldn't have been more at odds with Michael's mood. It had been a bad start to the work day. What was the use of putting his heart into his work, he asked himself, if the top guns funding it all always had the final say? Was it still possible, in 1996, for an intellectual to make art? Michael, who usually socialized with everyone on the set, trotted down the studio's outdoor paths without a glance in their direction, nervous as a racehorse waiting for the gate. He walked straight ahead, not knowing toward what. An unsmiling Bruckheimer came to join him.

"Bad news," began the producer.

"Isn't it always?" asked Michael.

"They're still not happy upstairs. There's a lot of pressure to dumb down the movie's underlying concepts."

"I know, I just met with the kiss-asses working for the studio. They're a couple of hotheads, real intellectual charlatans," Michael fumed.

"Simpson is trying to handle the situation, but it's a difficult discussion given our opponent's tainted logic."

"Their accusations are unfair. All they want is drama."

"I know. It's not looking good, but try to have confidence in Don. He is the wiser of us two, even though he likes, ironically some might say, to claim the opposite. It's only an act," said Bruckheimer.

"By the way, was it his idea to hire Connery? He's impossible to work with."

"Don saw something in him."

"All I've seen is his skill for disrupting the shooting schedule."

"Yes, about that, I meant to say... We have to stop filming for a few days. They have the movie rights. Our hands are tied. Take a few days off."

Michael bristled with anger.

"What?! Not only do they sully our ideal, now they want to keep us from working? Imbeciles!"

"It's politics, Michael. Let Simpson do his job."

"I'm taking the rest of the day off, but I'll be back here at 5:30 tomorrow morning."

Michael left the set as Bruckheimer looked on with concern. He would try to make the most of the day. On a picnic table near the front desk, a copy of the latest issue of *People* caught his eye. Printed across a photo montage was the patently false headline "Michael Bay and Daphné Back Together."

ON THE DESIRE TO MEND FENCES

LIKE MICHAEL, the Apollo gym had seen better days. The film director parked his yellow Ferrari near the abandoned building. Then he walked over to the grimy window and peered through the glass, trying to make sense of the dusty exercise machines. It was late afternoon and the street was quiet. The gym, which gave every appearance of being a former Bay area bodybuilding hotspot, wasn't far from the Castro Theater; in the distance, Alcatraz Island sparkled in the middle of the water, the Golden Gate Bridge to its left. It had been six months since the *Bad Boys* premiere. Michael hadn't heard from Detective Hummel since. The investigation into the Miami incident had been put on hold for lack of progress.

Michael couldn't stand being in the dark any longer.

He had therefore insisted, during preproduction, that his second film be shot in San Francisco, where he could simultaneously carry out his own investigation. He was determined to unlock the mystery and in so doing secretly hoped to win back a certain beautiful PhD student. Only Michael soon realized the few investigative tools he'd garnered from the detective novels he'd devoured since childhood were of little use in the real world. It was his seventh visit to the Apollo, and he seemed to be running on a treadmill, headed nowhere. He took a few steps back to view the building's entire façade, then inspected his surroundings. Business was clearly booming on the strip, if the numerous cafes, hair salons, saunas, and nightclubs were anything to go by. Yet the gym lay in ruins. The property's sad state—the peeling paint, its rusted sign and overturned appliances, the feral fauna, the encroaching vegetation—suggested the establishment had been abandoned for some time, perhaps even years. Why hadn't another business swooped in on this stellar location? And why had the vandals, so active elsewhere in the city, overlooked this specific locale? At the street corner, among the passersby, a man stood half hidden behind a wall, a telephoto lens aimed straight at Michael. A wave of heat swept over Michael as the blood rushed to his head.

"Fucking hell," he muttered, livid.

With a determined look on his face, Michael rushed straight toward the photographer, who'd picked a bad day to follow him. Caught in the act, the man froze for a moment, then took off down a cross-street. Michael ran faster, shouting at the photographer to stop, even though the man had already disappeared from sight. Just before the intersection, the sudden roar of an engine caused

Michael to slow his step. A deafening crunch of metal rang out as a black Hummer zoomed through the intersection, slammed into a stack of orange crates, sending fruit flying, and crashed into a taxi that had just turned onto the street. The beast of a vehicle, barely slowed by the crash, kept going as the taxi flipped several times and landed on some chicken cages, which exploded into a thousand delicate floating feathers.

Michael was not in a forgiving mood. He doubled back to his Ferrari as fast as he could, its ignition jumping to life with typically Italian zeal. The photographer may have had brawn on his side, but Michael had style.

Hurtling down the steep city slopes, making up in presence what it lacked in precision, the Hummer sped toward downtown San Francisco. At each plateau, the Hummer flew several feet into the air, landing on other vehicles here and there as it sent up a shower of sparks and crushed them like little toy cars. In its path, what had once been individual objects now lay indistinguishable in a heap of rubble. Michael's yellow Ferrari F355 Spider tried to catch up to the Hummer, but was slowed by the debris, forcing it to put its razor-sharp responsiveness to good use. Michael handled the wheel and stick with confidence, his body becoming one with the supercar. A sudden surge of affection for his adoptive father caught him off guard. He remembered their regular visits to the Van Nuys Speedway—the good-natured passes and combative skids. He put the thought out of his mind. Further down the hill, the Hummer soared through the air and collided with a tractor trailer hauling a few hundred gallons of water. In the distance, through the multicolor mist that sprayed through the air, San Francisco looked beautiful—the skyscrapers of the city center, the magnificent Transamerica Pyramid, its slender white point basking proudly in the warm light, evoking all the glory of the United States of America. On the Ferrari's rear bumper, a "Support Our Troops" sticker served as a reminder of what was important.

The roadway now obstructed by hundreds of cracked plastic gallon water jugs, Michael had to think fast. He took the first left and then a sharp right, careening wildly down a back alley. The obstacles weren't quite as numerous—garbage bags, bins, wood pallets, cats—but the space to maneuver proved as narrow as the adjusted waistlines of his father's clients. More determined than ever, Michael shifted gears and sped through the alley, ripping open several garbage bags to reveal their contents to the local homeless population.

For optimal efficiency, Michael concentrated on his immediate surroundings and let his driving reflexes take care of the rest. He could see an enormous obstacle up ahead, but it was difficult to make out. Squinting into the distance, he realized he was headed at sixty-five miles per hour toward an enormous dumpster blocking the alley. Even at its current speed, there was no way the Ferrari would be able to plow through it. The distance separating the two objects burned up before his eyes like a flaming fuse. Michael suddenly heard the whine of another engine, more nasal this time, reverberating in the alley: above, he saw Nic Cage's princely silhouette bounding across the rooftops on a dirt bike.

Cage dropped a sturdy wood pallet down into the alley, where it landed on an angle, one side leaning against a stack of milk crates. With any luck, it would be at just the right angle to serve as a launch pad for the Ferrari. Braking was never an option: Michael gunned the engine and flew into the air. All he had to do now was sit back and admire the view, carried forward by the laws of ballistics. The alley was surprisingly picturesque. Its walls were covered in bright colors, stylized signatures—for the most part territorial markings—alongside urban artworks in a remarkable mix of the trivial and the sublime. Here, spray paint had continued to create meaning, year after year. The walls of the Californian alley, from his bird's eye view, were palimpsests whose surfaces artists and hoodlums constantly competed for, subverting, with varying degrees of finesse, the marks left by their most recent predecessors. "Genette was right," thought Michael, who'd always promised himself he'd one day explore the cinematic possibilities of transtextual relationships. While he wanted to tackle them all, he admittedly had a soft spot for hypertextuality, seeing each new work as a potential hypotext.

One detail of the jumbled fresco in particular caught his attention: Alcatraz, encircled by unidentified men, their backs to the island. It looked like something Eric

Drooker, a frequent cover artist for *The New Yorker*, might have dreamed up. The sparse aerosol lines evoked a striking feeling of isolation. Michael saw himself in the drawing and felt, for a few brief moments, suffused with the gift of clairvoyance. He'd written the draft script for *The Rock* very quickly, full of inspiration, letting his superego run as unbridled as possible. *The Rock* was a laboratory, a place to reflect, but also a place to express himself. He would be lying if he claimed to fully understand the significance of all the elements he'd brought together in his early vision. But from that moment on, the choice of Alcatraz as a backdrop would come to symbolize for him the ostracism he felt he was a victim of. True, Simpson and Bruckheimer seemed to believe in him, but his confidence in these rare allies had now been compromised. Everyone else had rejected him: the studio he worked for did not acknowledge his intellectual authority, the university ignored him, and Daphné considered him a fraud. Perhaps the latter two would change their minds once they'd seen his new film. After all, the hero, played by Cage, was a scientist and an academic. Michael even thought fleetingly of Danny, his one true friend, and to whom, for reasons that had long remained unclear, he hadn't spoken in years. Since the Clio awards ceremony, in fact, when Michael had received the highest distinction. Danny had come to congratulate him afterward. During their conversation he'd announced, with his signature false modesty, that he'd received a prestigious grant for his doctoral work, which was already turning influential heads. Michael, whose work the industry was acknowledging at that exact moment, had been filled with a kind of profound listlessness, a feeling that he now understood, as he soared through the air in a back alley of layered meanings, to be jealousy. Though not yet clear to Michael during that post-event cocktail reception, the young man he'd loved was no longer a brother, but a rival. Although Michael hadn't cut his ties to Danny cleanly or transparently, likely because he was ashamed of his jealousy, likely because he didn't want to acknowledge an egocentrism that made him incapable of celebrating the success of others, Michael had simply neglected the relationship. He'd responded less and less frequently to Danny's invitations, which eventually dried up, only adding to his solitude.

The Ferrari was falling fast, its shocks about to be put to the test. But as the stretch of alley approached its end, Michael became increasingly aware of the imminent landing that would occur not in the relative security of the backstreet, but in the middle of the busy intersecting avenue just ahead. In the frame created by the walls on either side of the alley, just feet from the Ferrari's nose, vehicles appeared and disappeared again—left, right, right, left. Michael clamped down on the wheel and gritted his teeth.

As people on the busy street looked on in astonishment, the alley spat out a yellow vehicle, which soared weightlessly through the air as the tank-like Hummer sped down the road. The choreography of events to come would top even the chase scene in *The Rock*: the Ferrari crashed down into the back of the Hummer, forcing it to admit defeat. Stunned by the impact, the photographer stopped for a few seconds in the middle of California Street, fragments of the vehicle's shattered back window scattered across the backseat. Michael didn't fare much better; his airbag had deployed after the Ferrari's nearly 360° semi-aerial spin. To avoid the two vehicles now blocking the road, several panicked drivers attempted sharp turns or stopped without warning; one car swerved onto the sidewalk and hit a telephone pole which, like a tree during the colonization of the New World, toppled heavily onto the street, sending two or three unsuspecting vehicles flying. Stunned onlookers took in the sight of a near-perfect illustration of the word "pileup."

The photographer reacted first, still determined to flee. Peering over the airbag pinning him to the seat, Michael saw the banged-up Hummer disappear toward downtown. There was no time to lose if he wanted to keep him in sight. He'd have to puncture the airbag—but with what? There were no sharp objects within reach. Short on time and options, Michael grabbed his pistol, the American version of a Swiss army knife. A sharp but satisfying pain pierced his eardrums, and he regained mobility. He slammed his foot on the accelerator, thrust the car into gear and, before following the Hummer down California Street, spun the vehicle a few times on the asphalt, leaving behind a few swirls of rubber and an epic trail of white smoke—a show of virility cheered by even the most bruised and battered drivers trapped inside the heap of scrap metal.

The shops blurred past on either side of the bumble-bee-yellow sports car as it raced down California Street, one of San Francisco's main thoroughfares that, while not its most emblematic, certainly embodied its renowned hilliness. In the distance, the Oakland Bay Bridge sparkled amidst a canyon of business district buildings, an eternal runner-up linking peninsula and continent. Michael didn't know exactly what he would do with the photographer once he caught up to him; he wouldn't kill him—he was a director, not a psycho-path—but he had to find a way to stop him, or at least to make him reconsider his life choices. What a parasitic career! What a despicable profession! Like the rearing stallion affixed to his steering wheel, Michael was ready to charge. Tolerance, a value that had been instilled in Michael from the earliest age, was yielding to an irri-tation he was increasingly sure stemmed from a thirst for revenge. Then it occurred to him: he couldn't care less if the tabloids spread fake rumors about him; in fact, he quite enjoyed the attention. The only rational explanation for his irrational behavior lay, no doubt, in a futile desire to rewrite the events of that evening at the Chinese Theater, in a posteriori attempt to neutralize the sources of stress that had tainted Daphné's receptivity. His darling Daphné, ordinarily so reserved, had clearly not enjoyed being the center of attention. No doubt the incessant flashes had dazed her. Take away Mary Hart and the paparazzi, and Daphné would likely have grasped all the theoretical depth of *Bad Boys*. The man Michael now pursued was, by association, responsible for his emotional distress. How good it would feel, once he neutralized the Hummer, to grab the photographer by the throat, throw him against a wall, and unleash a stream of arguments into his voyeuristic face that would erode the man's most fundamental certainties!

Just as he began mentally rehearsing his diatribe, the car's semi-portable phone, an extra he'd opted for upon purchase, rang loudly. Despite the call's poor timing, Michael picked up the receiver attached to the dashboard via a coiled cord.

"This isn't really a good time," began Michael. "Can I call you back?"

"End this chase," replied an unfamiliar, accented voice. "You'll gain nothing."

"Who is this? How did you get this number?"

"I don't wish you any harm. The people I work for don't wish you any harm. If you keep following me, you'll only hurt yourself."

"What?! You're the guy in the Hummer? Pull over right now! And I'll ask you again: how did you get this number?"

"The people I work for know many things."

"They don't seem to know much about respect for people's private lives! Who are you working for? *National*

Enquirer? People? Star Magazine? Do you take pleasure in ruining the lives of hard-working Americans?"

"One day you'll thank me. But for now I'm just a shadow."

"What? What are you talking about? What does all this mean?"

"The question you should be asking is: what is meaning?"

A dial tone indicated the photographer had ended the call. Michael had no time to reflect on the mystery: just as he managed to catch up to the Hummer again, he saw it swerve abruptly and hit the back of a cable car full of tourists that was gently descending the hill. The red, ochre, and burgundy cable car, ordinarily a calm and picturesque mode of transportation, derailed and began sliding down the hill sideways. The Hummer accelerated and managed to overtake it, satisfied with its strategy. Michael tried to do the same, but panicked passengers had begun leaping from both sides of the street car, rolling onto the pavement to cushion the fall, their faces showered with sparks from the steel wheels screeching against the macadam. The Ferrari swerved onto the sidewalk to avoid the passengers, who'd at least had time to get to their feet and dive out of the way. The car plowed into a row of parking meters, and a hail of shiny coins flew sparkling into the air. Now side by side with the cable car, Michael glanced inside. It was empty save for the driver, or "gripman" as they're known in San Francisco, who remained at the helm, ready to go down with his vessel. Michael was moved by the man's devotion. He passed the cable car nonetheless, realizing, once back on the sloping pavement, that the Hummer was gone.

The photographer must have turned down Grant Avenue, Chinatown's major artery. He could get to it at the next turn. His hand ready to yank the handbrake and skid the Ferrari around the corner, Michael felt a pang for the cable car operator, who he imagined hauling on his emergency brake too, only in vain. Though he needed to pay attention to the road ahead to safely complete his maneuver, Michael couldn't resist a quick look in the rearview mirror: the cable car was about to plow into a row of parked vehicles. Distracted by his poorly timed surge of empathy, Michael failed to notice the traffic light at the intersection ahead had just turned red. One after the other, some of them tossing a ball back and forth, the members of a wheelchair basketball team crossed California Street, too engrossed in the ball to see the Ferrari heading straight for them. Michael noticed the group just in time and swerved left to avoid them; the Ferrari responded well, so well that once the vehicle became perfectly perpendicular to the road it was hurtling down, the centrifugal force sent it into a series of aerial flips. Flashes of sky and asphalt tumbled in front of Michael's eyes through the driver's window. Through the dizziness, he could see he'd avoided causing further injury to the athletes he was now flying over. Almost at that exact moment, the cable car hit a station wagon, which exploded on impact. The powerful blast and resulting column of fire projected the station wagon more than sixty feet into the air, silencing the awe-stricken saxophone players busking on the street, their breathless melodies having, until that point, served as a stirring soundtrack to the carnage.

The Ferrari hit the ground first, the hood and top taking the brunt of the fall. Trapped upside-down in his now unusable sports car, Michael struggled to regain his senses as the dim glow of the interior light seemed to be drowning in a puddle of blood that continued to spread. The cable car, after floating for several seconds in the California skies, crashed heavily onto its side halfway down the hill and continued its descent with renewed aggression. Rattled, Michael sat powerless in the middle of the intersection where his car had just come to a stop. He shook his head, stretched his jaw, blinked several times, and realized as he watched the cable car slide toward him that his time had probably come. As he hung upside-down, he tried to unbuckle the seatbelt with his right hand, more out of instinct than anything else, but the mechanism was jammed. For a brief moment he considered using his hand gun to deal with the nylon strap like he had the airbag, but dismissed the idea, and in any case he had no idea where the gun was. He looked back at the cable car, which was getting bigger by the second. He exhaled through his nose, relaxed his body, and closed his eyes. This time, however, the prospect of his impending death failed to send him into a soothingly lucid state. The only thought that crossed his mind was "I've wasted my life."

Less than a hundred feet from oblivion, a strange whistling sound cut through the increasingly loud screech of wood and metal against asphalt, as though something were speeding toward him from behind. A strong smell of bergamot once again filled his senses; suddenly he felt the hot summer sun on his face, caressed by a sea breeze blowing in from a distant place. His hands were chubby and smooth, his view of the world a low-angle shot. He felt an inexplicable urge to move, crawling clumsily through the grass toward a ring of orange trees, drawn by a mysterious force. Once he'd gone past the trees, he felt something change, he felt uneasy. Then, after a few moments of confusion and darkness, he felt hot, very hot. The calm of the orange grove gradually gave way to the ambient noise of screams, cries, and combustion. A baby, dressed in a simple cotton diaper, he sat on the asphalt as everything around him burned, exploding, melting, dying. But he found the scene more fascinating than terrifying, the dancing flames choreographed by the tanker truck evoking more the festive atmosphere of a French cancan than the disturbing aura of a voodoo ritual. He was excited, his attention constantly diverted by a new detail of the scene, his hyperactive gaze, incapable of contemplation, endlessly jumping from one element to another. He saw people running as they were consumed by flames, others administering CPR to no avail or signaling their position to hypothetical first responders by setting off incandescent flares into the smoke-filled skies. He saw helicopters up above, fire trucks clearing a path as they plowed through the skeletons of cars, jets of water evaporating before reaching the fire they were meant to neutralize, dogs barking or licking their singed fur. He also noted, off to the side, a man whose lack of panic seemed out of place, and who, at that precise moment, appeared to be taking his picture. Could the waning light be affecting his vision? The screech of buckling sheet metal drew his attention upward, and Michael watched in amusement as an enormous transmission tower, one of its four legs damaged moments earlier by a second explosion, lurched in his direction with the clear intention of smashing everything in its path. As the noise grew louder and the monstrosity drew closer, Michael, rather than run, threw his head back, laughing, and applauded. Seconds before the tower crashed to the ground, he felt himself being grabbed under the arms, hoisted into the air as though he were flying, and set down several feet away, safe near what was now a giant mass of misshapen metal. He was no longer alone: the person who'd saved his life squeezed him tightly in a protective grasp, his head rested against a woman's soft, ample breast. Michael didn't resist. He could hear his savior's heart pounding through fabric and flesh. After a moment, certain that the threat had passed, the woman detached him from her bosom and lovingly caressed his cheeks with her thumb, wiping away the soot from his face with a bit of saliva. "Don't be afraid. We're going to take care of you," she told him. Despite her singed hair, her dirt-filled wounds, and the fact that she was covered in the blood of others, Harriett was beautiful amid the chaos, as though infused with a new mission that filled her with meaning. Feeling uncomfortable, Michael suddenly came to.

Almost nothing remained of the cable car. A few bits of burning wood were strewn about and a thick dark smoke rose from the flames, signaling to the furthest reaches of the city the location of the explosion that had been heard far and wide. Amid the rubble, the gripman, who'd somehow survived, mourned the loss of his vehicle as though it were a loved one. He brandished a fist at the sky and cursed an F-18 fighter jet that was now one missile short. In its cockpit, still blitzed and still dressed in red suspenders, only now sporting a pair of night-vision goggles, Sean Connery gave Michael the thumbs up as he tore through the clouds.

ON THE DESTINY OF VISIONARIES

THE SHOOT WAS DRAWING to a close. The requests for rewrites had never let up, and it was still unclear how the film would end.

How to finish the story? At first, the idea had been for Cage and Connery's characters to spark an intellectual revolution: academic knowledge and the wisdom of the Ancients would be thrust onto citizens of the world as the most reliable tools to solve any problem. The world would be saved, in keeping with Hollywood standards. But now it seemed the studio wanted to limit the scope of this message, for reasons that escaped all reason.

A banquet had been organized in an empty room of the Alcatraz prison. Disney had not been invited. Simpson and Bruckheimer gathered a small group together around a fine assortment of dishes to reflect on various options to bring the narrative to an end. One after the other, the guests weighed in on the issue, the flow of ideas uninterrupted but for one gentleman's persistent hiccupping. When all had presented their arguments, Bruckheimer moderated a respectful debate. Alcohol flowed, lubricating the exchange, so that soon the meeting's initial goal began to disappear from view.

Michael moved away from the group after the impromptu arrival of several inebriates who managed to derail the discussion for good. Though Simpson had been single-handedly managing relations with the studio's emissaries for several weeks now, Michael's mind was no more at ease. He was still concerned, plagued by their mutual headache. "What is meaning?" he kept asking himself. The car chase with the mysterious photographer a few weeks earlier had only served to further unsettle him. Numerous sources of stress swirled together in Michael's mind, which had become increasingly prone to making dubious connections. Like Meat Loaf, his brother in arms, he had trouble seeing the world as something other than a coherent system whose parts were in some way or other interrelated. Yet how could he explain the photographer's intentions in light of recent events? How could the man claim to wish him well when he represented precisely what had chased Daphné away? Why did he seem to speak in riddles? Was it significant that he had been spying on him at the precise moment Michael had been investigating the kidnapping? Was he really a member of the paparazzi? Did he have a lightning-bolt tattoo hidden beneath his shirt? Or was he part of the Tarantino and Sorkin cohort? Why was the studio trying its utmost to throw up roadblocks at every turn? Could he win Daphné back? Why couldn't he forget her? What had caused his birth parents to abandon him? What is meaning?

Too distracted to appreciate the sumptuous spread before him, Michael grabbed a few canapés and devoured them pensively. Suddenly he breathed in a great gulp of air that took him by surprise. The oxygen didn't seem to reach his lungs—or at least he felt the need to take another breath straightaway, to no avail. "Great," thought Michael, "now I'm having a psychosomatic reaction."

Formulating this hypothesis regarding his present state did not, however, help in the least, nor did it slow the unpleasant change in pressure in his respiratory system. Could Daphné's absence really be causing this level of discomfort? His throat swelled, blocking his trachea. Behind him, the festive gathering continued on, heedless of Michael's increasingly odd behavior. He backed up against the wall and brought his hand to his throat: his lymph nodes were undeniably inflamed. These were clearly not the effects of melancholia: he was having an allergic reaction.

His vocal chords compressed by the swelling, Michael was unable to call to his colleagues for help. Their silhouettes grew blurry. Isolated from the world now more than ever, alone in the face of adversity, he tried to focus, not to panic. A few feet away, the tray of canapés he'd eaten from grew equally indiscernible. He nonetheless cursed its undeniable sesame content. His senses dilated, growing spongy and imprecise. His eyes rolled back, offering an image of the world reminiscent of Monet's most abstract cathedrals. His legs gave way and he fell to his knees, disappearing almost completely behind the buffet. His nervous system was the next to go. His limbs stiffened and writhed as if in the throes of an epileptic fit as his face contorted into a shockingly hideous grimace.

Michael noted between gasps that there appeared to be a commotion on the other side of the room. Finally! They'd noticed he was in peril! Surely now help would arrive. Flu-like symptoms left him unsure whether he was hot or cold. Beads of sweat formed at his forehead and on his arms, but he shivered uncontrollably. He had the troubling feeling that a chill was creeping from his toes up through his legs. "If this cold goes any higher," he thought, "it'll be the end of me." But his head and face were red-hot; though probably delirious, he could have sworn he felt his lips chapping and cracking, and mounds of hives bubbling up on his cheeks.

What was taking so long? Why had no one come, even just to wait by his side for the ambulance? Had the panic in the room not meant they feared for his life? He tried once more to concentrate, squinting as best he could. The merrymakers were indeed gathered together, but they were still on the other side of the room, engrossed in another incident. The glacial numbness reached his thighs and took hold of every muscular fiber. Michael tried one last time to make a sound so that someone would notice, but only managed to choke.

Doubled over on his knees, Michael could feel he was about to pass out, poisoned by his own carbon monoxide. Dying this way was too idiotic. He still had so many things to accomplish, so many questions to ask, so many bridges to mend. He'd have to find the strength to keep fighting, the strength to survive this ordeal. Then he'd have to follow his instincts and, as he always did, look to his own life for the inspiration to end *The Rock*. Once the film was done, he would finally have some time to himself and could return, for the first time in years, to Orange County, where all his memories seemed to lead. He couldn't die without finding out who he was, where he came from, the reason for his existence. Trembling and sweaty, he slowly reached his right hand down his pant leg and lifted up the cuff. He felt around for the cylindrical object tucked between his sock and his ankle. He tried to grasp it but his hand wouldn't cooperate, clenching and relaxing like Dostoyevsky on a bad day. As the cold gradually reached his hips and he imagined the boils on his face bursting, Michael managed to nudge down his sock and grab the enormous syringe. With superhuman effort, he raised the Epipen up at arm's length in front of him, activated the mechanism to release the frighteningly large needle, gaped at the point—and especially at its length—and with two hands, thinking only of Daphné's face, plunged it directly into his heart.

Michael lost his balance and collapsed onto his side, convulsing violently, the needle still planted in his chest.

His eyes were wide open, almost too wide. The adrenaline rushed through his veins and he was soon able to take a genuine gulp of air. The oxygen provided almost as much relief as the contents of the syringe. The spasms that had wracked his entire body became less frequent and, though his heart pumped furiously, he felt calm. Slowly he rolled over onto his back, stretching his arms out to each side in a Christ-like pose to ease his breathing. Feeling gradually returned to his legs like a kind of effervescence, but he was still not fully lucid. Everything seemed to move in slow motion, even the drops of sweat that continued to bead and slide down his forehead. The spasms rattling his chest became weaker. Sounds were still muffled, but he thought he heard someone from across the room call over, "The ambulance is on its way! I hope it's not too late!" His eyes now half-closed, he stared at the white ceiling of the banquet hall trying to make sense of what was happening. If they'd called an ambulance, then why hadn't anyone come over to help? Everyone still seemed nervous and it looked as though some of the men might even be crying.

Slowly, Michael turned his head toward the group. He blinked a few times so his eyes could focus. His dilated pupils returned to their usual diameter. Everyone still had their backs to him. He tried to call for help again, but was only able to produce a feeble kettle-like hiss. How could he get the crowd's attention if he could barely move, his body exhausted by the very effort of survival? On the ground near his head, he noticed one of the hors d'oeuvres that had set off his allergic reaction. He now saw what he'd failed to notice before: that it was a piece of bruschetta. Michael was no chef, but his few trips to Italy had taught him that sesame had no place in that particular appetizer.

Two paramedics appeared and headed straight toward the group at the far side of the room. Michael struggled with the left pocket of his cargo pants to find something to get their attention. Another cylindrical object came to his aid. He pulled it out and feebly knocked one end against the floor. The small flare sent thousands of sparks flying, filling the room with a thick green smoke.

"I got green smoke!" yelled one of the paramedics. To Michael's great relief, the man, elegantly dressed in a crisply-pressed uniform, ran over to check his vitals. The group of thinkers stirred again. Michael was helped to his feet and wrapped in a military blanket. With the paramedic's help, the syringe still lodged in his chest, Michael managed to take baby steps over to his now-sober colleagues. "He's been poisoned!" said some, while others, clearly in a less coherent state, cried, "We owe a cock! Don't forget to pay the cock!" to whoever would listen. Michael was confused. The shoot was certainly heading downhill fast.

The paramedic tried to rush him outside to administer care in relative calm, but Michael stopped in his tracks when he got to the site of the drama that had rivaled his own. In the middle of the crowd, a second paramedic was hunched over someone, administering powerful chest compressions. Michael was stunned. A wave of nausea swept over him. He strained his neck to the right, then to the left, driven by the kind of morbid curiosity that causes traffic jams after a highway pileup. A sheer covering obscured part of the face of the man lying there. The paramedic delivered a few final chest compressions, then the muscles of his neck relaxed in surrender. He stood back up. Now Michael had a clear line of sight. Lying on the stone floor, eyes unmoving, body frozen mid-convulsion in a mannerist position, his index finger pointing to the sky, Don Simpson hadn't managed to stop the cold from reaching his heart.

"He's dead," pronounced the paramedic, as he reached down and closed Simpson's mouth and eyes.

ON THE EVOCATIVE POWER
OF ORANGE TREES

MOMENTS BEFORE STARS filled the sky, the sandy ground itself seeming to give off a pale rosy light, Michael Bay's old Dodge Ram sped down an Orange County backroad trailing a long cloud of dust. Far in the distance, the Pacific Ocean soaked up the remains of the day, and ahead, above the steep stony mountains known to locals as Old Saddleback, the first Perseids of the year lit up the sky, majestic and graceful, their destructive power eclipsed only by their splendor.

The gravel crunched under the truck's tires as Michael braked in the driveway. He stared into space for a few minutes, both hands on the wheel, then summoned the courage to turn off the ignition, open the door and, for the first time in a long time, stepped out onto the property in his designer cowboy boots. At first glance, everything looked the same. The old wind pump still creaked, a faded American flag still fluttered above the steps. From the outside, it was difficult to tell whether Harriett and Jim continued to visit the country house regularly, or if they'd abandoned it, saddened at how empty it felt, so unlike the days of his childhood when he would run around the place, his model space shuttle held high in the air. The building's neglected appearance—no doubt intentional—contrasted with the newer, flashier design of the modern and impressively large white house. There was something authentic about the country home. It was the kind of place you'd wear jeans. There was a wraparound veranda where you half expected to see Hank Williams serenading a pack of rapt coyotes. The property extended out onto a rolling acreage that boasted a small artisanal orange grove, a large crater that filled with water during rare periods of heavy rainfall, wooden fences that had no doubt once, well before the Bays moved in, penned in a herd of livestock, as well as a cactus-covered butte perfect for hunting lizards. If you squinted hard enough, you could make out the oil fields beyond the property limits, where Jim had apprenticed on the rigs to pay his way through college.

The front door was locked. It's probably for the best, thought Michael, who had, after all, made the journey solely to search for the part of his identity contained within the fruit trees. But it was hard to resist a quick visit to this place full of memories. Forcing the door was out of the question. Michael didn't want to leave behind any trace. If memory served him right, the window to his upstairs room didn't lock. With a bit of climbing, he could probably get in that way. Michael grabbed onto the drainpipe at the side of the house and managed to hoist himself up with surprising ease. Through the window, the room was black as the night that had now descended. Had Harriett and Jim, in their grief, repurposed the room? What would he find on the other side of the pane? His science magazines or exercise machines? Michael focused on his breathing and, without further thought or effort, slid open the window.

Inside, silence reigned as if in a vacuum. In total darkness, save for the glowing constellations still glued to the ceiling, Michael inched slowly forward. His hand reached for the light switch, which his clammy fingers managed to turn. The furniture hadn't moved. In the corner stood his old bed, still covered with a duvet bearing Carl Sagan's likeness. His desk stood in the same place, as did the comfortable beanbag chair where he'd read many a book. The built-in bookshelf was still lined with his books and glass cases showcasing his exploits as an amateur entomologist. But what moved him most wasn't that the space had been preserved: the walls, once left bare to limit distraction, were now covered with posters, in various languages, of *Bad Boys* and *The Rock*, while the shelves held carefully labeled albums containing news clippings about him. And there was a new dresser in the room. Etched into its surface were the words *For Daphné*.

186

Under the bluish moon, Michael walked toward the orange grove, his mind in tumult. He wasn't quite sure what to expect. A soft wind swept across his face, and along with it came the scent he'd hoped to find, at once enveloping and full of answers. He tried, as much as he could, not to think of the shrine-like room devoted to his film career, almost-irrefutable proof of his ersatz parents' pride in him. He was here to uncover his true origins, not to reconcile with those who were in fact responsible for the mystery, as far as he was concerned. The problem was, he found it increasingly difficult to summon the feeling that had caused him to remain so immune, over the past twenty years, to the repeated extending of hands by those who had, after all, raised and loved him.

The trees in the grove looked almost out of place in the arid setting. A sickly-sweet smell rose up from the rotten fruit scattered across the ground, overpowering the delicate floral scent that had preceded them. It appeared that the orange trees, once carefully pruned by Jim and Harriett or some other seasonal worker, had been left untended. The soles of his boots sticky from the juice-laden soil, Michael tried to attune his senses to any fluctuation in his state, but noted no changes. He walked to the middle of the artificial oasis and stopped there, ready to finally understand. The air was cool, more dry than oceanic, and the trees were still. The minutes passed fruitlessly. It seemed the revelations wouldn't come that easily. What should he do? Was there more to it than just the location? Did he also have to create certain conditions? His plan contained significant flaws. Impatient, Michael returned to the house and then ran back to the trees with several items in his bag. With the focus of a voodoo priest, he balanced a pot on top of a few spoiled oranges, then took out an impressive string of firecrackers.

Excited and desperate, Michael lit the middle fuse and dropped the makeshift catalyst into the pot. Safety was the least of his concerns; he took a single step backward, not wanting to miss any of the action. As the flame neared the first of the firecrackers, he leaned slightly forward and threw open his arms as though to embrace the explosion. A sound like machine gun fire rang out through the night, waking hundreds of birds and sending them flying, panic-stricken and screeching, into the sky. The firecrackers went off at a furious pace. Michael, still feeling completely anchored in time and space, drew closer to the pot, trying to harness all the evocative power of the last few sparks. The heat sent one explosive shooting out of the pot. It flew through the air and slammed into Michael's chest, knocking him to the ground. The blasts grew fewer and farther between, soon replaced by the silence of the night. A thin wisp of grey smoke rose from the pot, curling for a moment into the shape of a question mark. Michael, his backside and hands covered in sticky orange juice, reflected on his failed plan, his failed hypothesis, his failed quest. Eyebrows arched and jaw quivering, he lowered his gaze and let out the sobs he had held back for so long.

It was a long walk back to the truck. Michael was at a loss. What could he do now? Visit all the orange groves in the country? That seemed a tall order and, given the state he was in, it would likely come to naught. Would he simply have to settle for not knowing? Should he consider this evening a sign it was time to make peace with the parents who'd rescued him from the scene of a burning oil tanker? Near the house, the family linden tree was still standing, more regal than ever, decorated with a string of small lights as if it were Christmas. The cord lay unplugged at the base of the tree. Michael paused, took a quick look around to be sure he was still alone, then plugged it in. Hundreds of little white lights sparkled on the tree. Michael took a few steps back and realized that the luminous shape, set against the darkness, resembled a mushroom cloud. For some reason the sight calmed him. He decided to stay for a while and stretched out on the ground near the tree, arms folded behind his head. The night rolled out, dark, quiet, and cool. He didn't want to close his eyes, didn't want to fall asleep. But overcome with fatigue and emotion, he let his mind drift to moments spent years earlier under this same leafy canopy. It was there Harriett would often find him in the afternoon. She'd take animal crackers, a favorite snack of his, and walk them across his bare belly, narrating the whole thing as if it were a National Geographic video. He recalled how he'd cherished those tender moments, as happy to learn about the reproductive cycle of the armadillo as he was to strengthen the familial bond he'd once thought indestructible. Michael sat up on his elbows and gave himself three or four little slaps on the cheek to wake up. Is it possible, he wondered, that someone else out there right now is experiencing this same feeling? He felt dizzy before the vastness of humanity, of the universe. He stood back up, unplugged the lights, and headed back to the Dodge Ram.

The Perseids hailed on, tracing ephemeral arcs of light across the cosmos. As he fumbled in his pocket for the remote starter, Michael felt one last surge of curiosity. What about the barn? He walked the fifty or so yards behind the house to the structure, which had weathered somewhat but was otherwise still intact. It was impossible to see anything through the barn's cracked boards. Michael wasn't quite up for climbing; and besides, he didn't know of any other way into the building. Feeling tired, he tried pulling the enormous sliding door to the left. Other than a bit of rusty resistance, it opened easily. Standing in the enormous entryway and peering through the darkness, Michael thought he could make out the silhouette he'd hoped to find. He instinctively grabbed for the chain of the barn's only lightbulb, and a dim and flickering glow filled the space. Before him, standing at least twenty feet tall, directly beneath a retractable skylight, the family telescope was as massive as in his most fantastical childhood memories.

It seemed that Jim, who'd introduced young Michael to the joys and mysteries of astrophysics, had never stopped scrutinizing the infinite universe. The barn was full of maps, handwritten notes, and theoretical works, the majority of which Michael himself had annotated. His heart warmed at the sight of the volumes by Sagan, Newton, Halley, Hubble, Einstein that he'd once devoured, fascinated by their desire to sum up the universe in a few mathematical formulas. Many moons ago he'd been passionate about the discipline that had long since been shunted aside by so many other subjects competing for his attention. Seeing the telescope reignited something inside him. The question that man in the Hummer had asked—What is meaning?—continued to eat away at him. Perhaps the answer was something cosmic? He'd often been advised to take a step back when approaching a seemingly unsolvable problem, and nowhere seemed a more appropriate place to do this than outer space. The thought, halfway between hypothesis and method, reassured him. He decided not to decide about Jim and Harriett before first studying the stars which, as they attracted and repelled each other, could no doubt teach him a great deal about the complex relationships between bodies of the same family.

His electronic planner emitted a quiet beep, reminding him of a production meeting several hours later at the Culver City offices. Don Simpson's death had shaken not only the company's administrative structure, but also its soul. Bruckheimer would try to take stock of the situation. More importantly, Michael was supposed to present an overview of his next film and he still wasn't sure what it would be about. The same idea kept cycling through his mind: Steve Buscemi as Casanova, a denunciation of superficiality. He'd likely run with that to buy some time. The hours till dawn kept slipping away, but Michael couldn't resist one last look through the giant telescope. The possibility of seeing a shooting star up close thrilled him. He activated the mechanism to open the roof, climbed the steps to the padded observation chair, made himself comfortable, his back at a slight angle to the floor, and leaned in close to the telescope. He hadn't made any calculations, so he wasn't quite sure what he was seeing through this lens that filmed nothing. Before the vastness, he felt like he was floating weightlessly amid the overcrowded void for a moment, outside of his body. The lens must have been damaged or dirty: a hazy object in the foreground made the image unclear. Michael tried to focus the lens and minimize the visual impact of the foreign body. The nature of the static soon became apparent. There was nothing obscuring the lens. In the telescope's direct line of sight, the *Atlantis* shuttle, mid-mission, lay between Michael and the Milky Way. Michael was surprised at the telescope's power, having never before used it to observe an object so close to Earth. He could see the shuttle very clearly now: its black nose contrasting with its white hull, a design more evocative of aviation than galactic exploration, its back open to reveal the Canadarm, itself connected to a satellite in the midst of repairs. An astronaut floated gracefully in the ether, tools in hand, putting numerous years of training to good use. Michael felt proud to be an American. Suddenly the shuttle seemed to rotate on its axis and Michael thought he saw debris fly from one of its wings. The astronaut let go and shot back from the satellite. A mysterious, fast-moving object hit the cable attaching the satellite to the Canadarm and immediately snapped it in two. The projectiles multiplied and the damage increased, as a meteorite shower pelted the powerless vessel. Debris hit the cockpit, then the tail and one of the engines. *Atlantis* exploded in silence as its oxygen reserves ignited in a puff of orange, which the void swallowed up in an instant.

ON THE EXTINCTION OF DINOSAURS

THE NASA HANGAR would have had room to spare for the biggest egos in Hollywood and Olympus. As a frenzied horde of journalists waited outside, the door lifted to reveal a few dozen men in space suits lined up with military precision, helmets under their arms. Owen Wilson appeared first, followed by Steve Buscemi, Ben Affleck, Will Patton, Bruce Willis, and Michael Clarke Duncan. Then came the actual astronauts. Hanging back at the end of the line stood Michael, who had also suited up, flanked by a few camera men, his soundman, several astrophysicists, and Jerry Bruckheimer.

Behind their seemingly stoic gazes toward the horizon, piercing through everything else with a truly patriotic solemnity, the heroes were tense, as excited as they were nervous. Outside the hangar, an impressive regiment of armed soldiers stood guard. On the tarmac, civilians were packed into bleachers, brandishing binoculars and signs and waving notebooks for autographs, their shouts superposed over the power ballads of Aerosmith, who were performing live on a stage nearby. Army helicopters circled above, backlit by the sunset. A red carpet had been rolled out in front of the door, parting the crowd and forming a path to the chrome bus that, any minute now, would take the group of astronauts to the three enormous launch sites towering over Cape Canaveral.

The event was broadcasting live on radio and TV in over thirty countries. Several networks had interrupted their regular programming for the historic launch, dubbed "Stars in the Stars" by certain influential newscasters. In France, Vietnam, Morocco, Arkansas, India, Quebec, and beyond, Willis and Affleck fans were glued to their devices, solemn and anxious to see their favorite celebrities launch into space in what would be the most audacious film shoot in cinematic history. For two weeks, according to a schedule that had been planned in great detail by a team of engineers, they'd be shooting *Armageddon*'s space scenes on location. Bruckheimer and Michael had made the decision after Michael, wealthier than ever after the box-office success of his first two films, offered to fund the launch of three space shuttles.

The explosion of *Atlantis* several months earlier had generated renewed interest in comets—a source of concern that dated back to when the first man had lifted his gaze to the night sky. Asteroid showers were usually an indication of a more imposing celestial body not far off, and this one was no different. Alerted by this ill omen, astrophysicists had spotted an asteroid the size of Texas speeding across the solar system, beating a dangerous path toward Earth. Despite attempts by the powers that be to keep the secret under wraps and avoid global panic, the news spread like wildfire. For the first time, humanity was facing the real and imminent threat of total eradication.

The prospect of the end dominated every conversation. Given the sudden futility of conflict, a sense of global brotherhood emerged. Television stations devoted precious primetime slots to programming on philosophical issues that would previously have tanked their ratings; people suddenly became more interested in giving meaning to their soon-to-be-cut-short existence than hearing about Hollywood's latest break-ups. This period of resigned harmony was, however, short lived. Based on new data, NASA scientists were able to calculate the trajectory of the asteroid with increased precision and found that it would, in fact, bypass Earth. The world exhaled, then went back to normal, with one small exception: comets, having been in the news so much, were now a hot topic.

Michael and the other astronauts posed for a few seconds, then made their way down the red carpet through the impromptu tunnel of honor formed by the sound booms held out by the journalists along either side. Accustomed to these outpourings of attention, the actors waved to the crowd, exhilarated by the incessant camera flashes and repeated shouts of their names, while the more reserved technicians and scientists tried to keep it together before the eager crowd. Michael looked handsome in his orange space suit, an American flag patch on his right bicep. Rarely had he felt so excited about starting a shoot, and it showed. His chest swelled with pride as his thoughts went back to the different facets of aerospace training he and his crew had received over the past weeks and which had culminated in this exact moment: supersonic flights to acclimate their bodies to the g-forces in space, zero gravity simulations, an introduction to the specialized tools and shuttle controls, familiarization with the different vital support systems, etc. Never had NASA worked with Hollywood so closely, which made Michael confident his third film would be well-received. Just like *Bad Boys*, *The Rock* had been completely ignored by academia. But Michael, despite a few moments of self-doubt (a necessary part of the creative process, he assured himself), hadn't given up. He felt his latest project was particularly well conceived: *Armageddon* would be a chance for him to reflect on his relationship with his adoptive parents, the mysteries of the cosmos, and the nature of meaning, as well as to attract the attention of the scientific community with his avant-garde methodology. Though historians and film theorists had thus far dismissed his work, the field of astrophysics was sure to take an interest in his project—meaning, without a doubt, that he would be the talk of the country's most prestigious college campuses. Film studies departments

197

would sit up and pay attention. Daphné would sit up and pay attention.

The chrome bus stopped near the three launch platforms, where a space shuttle was affixed in a vertical position to each. The actors would soon board the first two shuttles—*Liberty* and *Independence*—along with a handful of technicians and interplanetary navigation professionals. Bruce Willis would be the symbolic captain of *Liberty*, while Ben Affleck, his character an orphan desperate to prove his worth to his father-in-law, would lead *Independence*. The third shuttle—christened *Truth*—would serve as the research and production HQ. On board would be Michael, Bruckheimer, and a few operators brought along to capture the images, along with Dr. Tyson and his scientist colleagues, who would take advantage of the trip to verify certain hypotheses. The astronauts were now on the tarmac, their features blurred in the shimmer of the warm, oily air. In the distance, an Aerosmith song reached a crescendo as various emergency vehicles took position.

Truth's cabin was cramped but ergonomic. Its eight passengers silently squeezed in, face and torso turned skyward, while NASA technicians with grave expressions strapped them tightly into their seats. Night had fallen and a bluish light filtered through the shuttle's windshield, blending with the emerald glow of the control panel. More than a thousand miles away in Houston, Billy Bob Thornton rehearsed his lines at Mission Control Center, surrounded by a hundred men staring at monitors, answering phones, or checking off lists. An enormous screen on the wall showed a live feed of the reactors heating up, while vectors and data scrolled by on another. A third was broadcasting alternating images from each of the shuttles' cockpits: while Steve Buscemi received the final touches to his makeup, Ben Affleck leafed through the script, Owen Wilson whispered "She sells seashells on the seashore" over and over, and Bruce Willis, the quintessential method actor, squinted his eyes solemnly. The countdown to the triple launch read 00:10:00.

Michael activated his helmet mic and his voice echoed through the shuttles and over in Houston.

"Gentlemen, in a few seconds we'll be launching into space. I'm addressing you now not as a filmmaker, but as a man and humble member of the great brotherhood of humanity. Not long ago, we believed our world to be in danger of extinction. We were forced to imagine our lives cut short by a senseless event. We were forced to accept that we were powerless to help our loved ones. All that man has built, all that has been written for thousands of years, reduced to nothing by a random cosmic act. The news was difficult to swallow, but the human race has never been one to just sit back and wait. Some of us sought the comfort of our families. Others sought shelter in the writings of Kant, Heidegger, or Nietzsche. Still others fought back through acts of cre-ation, doubling their efforts to put the finishing touches on a long-neglected project that would justify, if only for a moment, their time on this Earth. I thought. I thought about humility—the lesson that the universe was trying to teach us. And I thought about conceit, about the arrogance of humankind and how, despite our smallness in the infiniteness of Things, we claim to understand. What can we really hope to know? What we believe today in 1996 to be the meaning of things is probably just an illusion, a hypothesis in the midst of being refuted. Did we learn nothing from Copernicus? From Galileo? From Bruno? What I retain from those great minds is the fundamental need for doubt. Our finest intellectual tools may prove to be mere nets that provide an illusion of safety in the face of unknown chaos. When we heard the Earth was saved, we were relieved. But what if that asteroid hitting us was an evil necessary in order to climb the ladder of consciousness? The dinosaurs that once walked this same Earth for millions of years were no doubt, in their own way, driven by this same arrogance, convinced that the expertise they'd gained over time would allow them to get the most out of their existence on Earth. No doubt held back by the limits of their consciousness, they couldn't have imagined their dominion one day modulated by poetry and science. But an asteroid trumped all those years of evolution, of perfected survival techniques, paving the way for a new and more advanced reign—that of humans. Who today would dare claim that dinosaurs were more intelligent than humans? An idiot, that's who. So we have to admit that man may not be the best the Earth has to offer when it comes to understanding the subtleties of existence. From what we know about the history of the world, it is possible to imagine that from the ashes of humanity new entities will arise that are more capable of producing real answers. I'm not saying I want to annihilate the human race (I'm not, as far as I know, a lunatic), but film provides a way to present this possibility, in an artistic manner, to our brothers and sisters. I say possibility, because it's still only a hypothesis. But we should never underestimate the power of an idea, especially one that can give rise to humility and doubt. Let's stop basking in the illusion of our grandeur. Ignorance is bliss, goes the old proverb. I'll add that bliss is laziness. And if you were selected for this mission it's because laziness doesn't sit well with you. I believe in every single one of you. Let's do this for humanity. May Don Simpson watch over all of us. Let's make him proud."

Seconds left to takeoff. On board *Liberty* and *Independence*, the men's eyes shone with inspiration. Michael gazed up at the stars, as Bruckheimer eyed him discreetly, approvingly, almost misty-eyed. Visors closed and locked according to protocol. The hull's vibrations increased. One by one, the operators in Houston confirmed their systems to be a go. Everything was set: they got the green light for launch. Boosters would fire up in ten seconds. The deafening roar of the engines all but drowned out the countdown, now being called out on board. On the ground, white smoke indicated the rush of oxygen from the propulsion system, as sparks shot out under the reactors and burned up the hydrogen. Five seconds. From the tail end of the first shuttle, still grounded, spat out three conical flames. Journalists and spectators around the world held their breath. Two. One. The sky suddenly filled with light as bright as day. *Liberty*'s two enormous booster rockets fired and the shuttle began its ascent, cloaking the ground in smoke and fire. Ten seconds later *Independence* followed, then *Truth*. Houston and Cape Canaveral exploded into shouts and applause.

When the vibrations abated, Michael Bay looked out and saw that he'd left Earth's atmosphere.

ON PATRIOTISM

COUNTLESS TRICOLOR PENNANTS undulate gracefully
in the Pacific wind along the streets of Honolulu. Amid
pineapple stands, floral garlands, and raffia skirts, masks
of the founding fathers pull in customers and line pock-
ets. The soldiers patrolling the streets excite the chil-
dren even more than the brightly colored mascots.
Bald-headed eagles are set free from their cages and
trace circles in the sky over the city's highest mountain
tops. Today, even traditional harpoons and blowguns
have been traded in for shiny firearms. Despite the distance separating the archipelago from the continent, the
feeling on the eve of the national holiday is decidedly
American.

Out of respect for their ancestors, the *Pearl Harbor*
crew has taken the day off.

The instant he sets foot on the University of Hawai'i
campus, Michael, once proud as a high-ranking officer,
keeps his head down, terrified of meeting a scornful
look. While he'd made it into a few scientific journals

with *Armageddon*, it was still solely as a counterexample. Jeanine Basinger had been the only one to add a dash of perspicacity, hailing the film in a publication for the prestigious Criterion Collection: "If he didn't work in Hollywood," she'd written, "Michael Bay would be the bad boy darling of the intelligentsia." Why then did the most influential academic figures enforce such a cruel dichotomy between Hollywood production and intellectual rigor? Was critical review doomed by its own tradition of operating solely within the framework of bad faith it seemed to have established as dogma? Basinger's kind words had failed to convince anyone, and Michael, not romantic enough to think himself a martyr, found it increasingly difficult to fight the fatigue, to fight the resignation about wanting to be known as a great creator of discourse. But two things continued to bolster his remarkable resilience: Daphné, obviously, Daphné, who he still dreamed of day and night, and also the possibility of making right on a career choice he'd long regretted. Years ago, interested but still inexperienced in the art of full-length features, he'd passed on directing *Saving Private Ryan*, which went on to win both statuettes and the esteem of the elite. *Pearl Harbor* represented his latest—and perhaps his last—chance to win over the Academy and take home an Oscar that would turn the right heads his way.

The social sciences library at UH Mānoa lacks some of the charm of its more elegant continental counterparts. Prefinished panels, vulgar angles, aggressive neon lighting, and worn carpets stand in lieu of colonnades, refined masonry, soft lighting, and noble materials. But its contents more than make up for its shortcomings in style. The library contains the United States' most comprehensive collection of works on the Second World War, particularly on the bombing of December 7, 1941. Once inside the institutional sanctuary, Michael steps aside so as not to block the entryway and searches for a sign indicating each floor's vocation. A pleasant scent of piña colada imparts a touch of class to the modest furnishings. The handful of students and employees in the building are barefoot. History shares the third floor with Fiction, according to a sign with sliding plastic panels near the main stairwell. Michael climbs the stairs two at a time. A few strides later and he's there, his heart pounding.

If *Pearl Harbor* is to be his historical masterpiece, his irreproachably factual homage to the American heroes who spilled their blood in the Oahu waters, he must press relentlessly on with his research—he must become an expert beyond compare. Before him stand ten entire rows dedicated to the Second World War, three of which thoroughly detail the 1941 Japanese attack. Walking along the rows in search of something different, one familiar volume catches his eye: *The World War II Combat Film: Anatomy of a Genre*. Despite the solemnness inherent to the place, Michael can't help smiling a little, for the first time in over a year. He would always have a place in academia even if it were due solely to this publication from his youth, this uncredited work in someone else's shadow. He would be part, unseen of course, but still part, of this select group he'd so long revered. But what if that period was in fact his pinnacle? If his creative and intellectual life were nothing more than a slow spiral down from the summit of his 19-year-old self? How long could he bear the systematic disappointment of those he so longed to impress? Michael, his face once again devoid of all joy, pulls out the book and holds it in his hands for a few moments, staring at where his name should appear on the cover of what seems to be his masterpiece by default. He instinctively leafs through the book, stopping in the middle of the chapter on *Tora! Tora! Tora!*, and recognizes one of his sentences pilfered word for word by the only professor who, ironically, still respects his work. Michael continues flipping the pages, the breeze making his lank hair flutter, and stops at the inside of the jacket cover, where a stamp in red ink marks May 9, 1989. Eleven years ago.

Drawn to the light as to oxygen from underwater, Michael steps away from the books to get some air at a nearby window. In the courtyard, technicians are installing a screen before a hundred folding chairs, in preparation for an ironic evening projection of *Top Gun* organized by one of the fraternities. Through the foliage of a Kukui nut tree, a man in black points a telephoto lens at Michael, who gives him the finger and mutters in painful, broken French, "Stick your *câlisse de* Kodak up your ass."

206

Wandering back to the books, Michael notices a poster on a bulletin board advertising an inter-university panel on the movies of James Cameron. The event is that day, at a pavilion not far from the library. On the program, among mostly unfamiliar names, he stumbles and stops short on one that strikes him like a blast mine: Daphné Couture, PhD, UCLA. According to the schedule, her presentation "King of the World: Self-Importance and Self-Indulgence in *Titanic*" has been in full swing for ten minutes. If he hurries, he might make the conclusion and manage to extrapolate the main arguments, ask a question to showcase his own vast knowledge as is custom, impress the audience, catch Daphné off guard, make his way through the crowd, climb on stage and yell dramatically, "I'm Michael Bay and I love this woman!", upend the table, grab Daphné in his arms, gain her enthusiastic consent, and kiss her to thunderous applause as he's showered with honorary PhDs. Michael glances at the main staircase, which is blocked by a group of Samoan students slowed by their substantial heft. Without wasting a second, he turns and runs straight at the open window, shielding his face with his arms. He hurls himself out into the courtyard greenery, shattering the glass as he goes. Shards soar through the air, surrounding him with a glowing halo, as witnesses to the scene see their faces reflected back in multiple fragments. Michael reaches out and manages to slow his fall by grabbing onto an orange scissor-lift platform occupied by a technician. The platform shakes and almost tips over, but Michael expertly shifts his weight to steady it. He hauls himself onto the platform next to the worker, who swears at him in Hawaiian, then leaps back into the air, this time toward the giant screen where a test for that evening's screening is projecting the aerial dance of a squadron of Tomcat F-14s. Mid-air, Michael reaches for his belt and unclips his vintage military knife, a movie shoot relic he'd taken a liking to. In one calculated gesture, he plunges the blade into the top of the screen, which tears from top to bottom under his weight, ripping Tom Cruise's helmeted head in two. He hits the ground running, each wasted second keeping him from basking in the sweet presence of a mind so brilliant, one that had managed nonetheless to plant doubt in his own. Under the nut tree, there's no sign of the photographer, who seems to have vanished into thin air. Some of the students waiting around for the movie screening boo Michael, who dodges a few harmless but distracting projectiles. One student recognizes him and yells, "Hey! Michael Bay! Your movies suck! Go back to Hollywood and keep feeding the stupidity machine!" The boos turn to scornful laughter. Michael tries to stay focused, but this new proof of institutional rejection turns his legs to jelly. There's a golf cart for campus maintenance staff parked on the paving stones just ahead. He jumps into the driver's seat and steps on the gas. The electric motor has nothing on the race cars lined up in his garage, but he is pleasantly surprised at how fast it accelerates. The campus is surprisingly busy, even though it's summer. While some students seem caught up in the intricacies of their summer courses, most appear to have their minds elsewhere. The further Michael gets from the quad, the denser the crowd gets. And the more its appearance changes—from the neat and tidy look that screams "serious student" to a more sports-inspired style, designer polos and briefcases giving way to numbered tees and foam hands. An annoying, nasal honk of the horn parts the surprised crowd like a biblical sea. Michael maintains his speed at all costs. Civilians fall to the sidewalk, as do their beers.

A sudden whiff of caramel popcorn grabs his attention: foot still on the gas, Michael looks up to see the college baseball stadium towering in all its grandiose solemnity above him. It's the first inning of a special game pitting the Honolulu Kaipukes against the Osaka Gyorai. A brief but vivid flashback overwhelms him, a jumble of ideas: conquest of land, experience of time, poetry, patriotism, and childhood afternoons, in the backyard of the modern and impressively large white house, Jim throwing baseballs, Michael launching them into the sky.

Michael's unfortunate tendency to daydream at top speed once again lands him in hot water: at the last second, he realizes he's headed straight for the ramp of a truck ferrying hot-dog stands. Powerless to stop, he clips the edge of one of the stands, drives onto the ramp and soars, at a distressing speed, through a spray of yellow mustard, into the perfectly blue sky. The trajectory of objects flying up from the ground now subject to the riotous pull of gravity, the vehicle's front wheels soon cease to point skyward and realign themselves, tracing the downward segment of an invisible arc toward one of the stadium walls, which, despite towering toward the heavens in a promise of infinity, wield nonetheless the threat of a brutal collision. Michael leaps out of the golf cart and lands with a graceful roll onto a patch of grass unscathed, as the abandoned cart rams into the wall and collapses in pieces onto a load of fireworks that explode into a glowing, popping bouquet. Thinking they'd missed a home run, a handful of inebriated fans erupt in rowdy cheers that, combined with the pyrotechnical display, bolster the morale of Michael, who's now just steps away from the pavilion where he'll find Daphné.

"... and that's why *Titanic*, though essentially a work created exclusively to feed Cameron's oversized ego, is still a film that will go down in history. Thank you."

Michael discreetly shuts the door of the dimly lit, sparsely filled auditorium behind him just as Daphné finishes her final sentence. The president of the event, an attractive, elegantly dressed older woman with vaguely Asian features, announces the start of the question period to an audience well accustomed to the order of things. Halfway to the microphone stand, Michael realizes the absurdity of his plan and stops short, still hidden in the shadows of the balcony. How exactly will a well-articulated question be enough to regain the trust of his love, who considers him an imposter? And what if, under pressure, he comes up with some unintelligent formulation? But most of all, how can Daphné show him affection, or even respect, before her peers whose esteem she craves and who, he knows only too well, despise him? He knows her to be ill at ease with university politicking, but that said, she's not entirely without pragmatism. The close presence of the woman he loved rendering him overly self-conscious and paralyzed with doubt, Michael takes a few steps back and sinks down into one of the seats in the last row, from which, like a spy or voyeur, he cranes his neck painfully to see her take her seat in the front row.

There's a bigger crowd at the cocktail reception than there was at the conference. Head lowered and shoulders hunched to shield his face, Michael had followed the group, from a slight distance, over to the student center serving as a bar for the evening. People help themselves to cheese, grapes, and pâté, but above all to copious amounts of wine. A glass of red in one hand, Michael plays the lone wolf, feigning interest in a collection of works on the shelves which, at that precise moment, hold nowhere near the attraction among the crowd as the bottles of alcohol. Hidden behind a shelf, he peers between the books and watches Daphné, who hasn't changed much since the last time he saw her.

Only her glasses are different: a bit bigger, a bit sexier. She's wearing an off-white blouse with a Peter Pan collar and a high-waisted black pencil skirt, her modest beauty as stunning as ever. It's like she's moving in slow motion as the room whirls around her, like in the Wong Kar-wai movie Michael can see a poster for out of the corner of his eye. He knocks back his wine.

After a few seconds, Michael realizes he's staring at her breasts. He catches himself trying to superimpose the memory of a topless Daphné on the shores of the Hudson River onto the Daphné standing before him. For the first time, it's not his heart or his mind that stirs at the sight of her, but his loins. Maybe he hadn't loved her as he should have. But he'd tried to do right by not falling into what he believed, perhaps naively, to be the trap of carnal union. He'd been taught to value intellectual love above everything; the love of ideas, a purer and, in the end, theoretically more lasting form of love than the vulgar collision of bodies. But maybe he had misread *Symposium*? He had been young when he read the formative work. Perhaps he hadn't known how to distinguish the different voices of dialogue, perhaps he'd attributed one argument to Plato when in fact he had championed the opposite? And hadn't it been Bruckheimer who'd introduced him to the love of the Forms all those years ago, to a type of understanding based on an experience of beauty? Michael adjusts his pants, cursing his youth and eroticizing Daphné's glasses. As he takes a few steps to the side to hide his obvious excitement, his feet hit something. On the ground, hidden from the view of most guests, a case of bottles lies waiting to replenish the current stock. Michael grabs one, opens it with his penknife, and fills his plastic cup.

Another thought makes his stomach churn: depending on how the next few hours unfold, this may be his last chance to see Daphné, to actually see her, in person, standing in front of him. He must calculate his move carefully. One false step and all hope of reconciliation is lost. At first, he stays where he is, hoping to keep the idea alive that this could all end well. He gazes at her, trying not to blink, carefully etching her precious image onto his retinas. Then, fearing he may one day forget, he grabs his phone and, well hidden behind a stack of books, snaps a few furtive photos of the woman who might never be his again.

A professor proposes a toast to the United States of America, the biggest, smartest, most beautiful country in the world. All enthusiastically raise a glass. Michael, who can't help joining in, puts his phone away, raises his glass, and presses his free hand to his heart. Corks pop loudly on a few bottles of Californian "Champagne" as its sweet and bitter foam splashes onto the bar. Bruce Springsteen blasts from a boom box on permanent loan from the audio-visual department. Even Daphné, who has been known to refer to her colleagues as jackals, seems to be having a good time among the pack of scholars.

Five glasses later, Michael tells himself it's time to take a break, or to at least drink some water. While he appreciates good wine, he is not in the habit of drinking himself numb. They say alcohol gives you courage, which is something he could do with right about now, but it's to the detriment of a mental sharpness that is usually his most effective weapon. Still alone behind a bookshelf, he loses sight of his objective for a moment and stares blankly at the posters decorating the walls: films directed by Godard, Fassbinder, Hitchcock, Cassavetes, Lang, Scorsese—works that seem to taunt him, reminding him of his own mediocrity. It's clearly time to leave.

"Michael, is that you?"

It's her. She's seen him. Mission compromised. Abort! Abort!

"Michael! It *is* you! Get over here and give me a hug!"

Without waiting for an answer, Daphné throws her arms around his neck, laughing. She squeezes him tight, stumbling a bit, which makes her laugh even harder. After an unusually long kiss on the cheek, she lets go, smiling, her gaze a bit hazy.

"What are you doing here? This is too funny! I mean... what? This is crazy! Haha! How long has it been? Three years? Four years? And you're still just as cute! Rrrawr! Haha!"

Michael didn't really have a plan, but if he did, this certainly wouldn't be part of it. He keeps quiet for a moment, flashes a dumb smile, then decides to act mysterious to gain a bit of time. In actual fact he looks more like one of those heroin addicts trying to earn a few dollars on a weekday morning on Hollywood Boulevard by doing a poor imitation of a statue.

"Seriously? You're not happy to see me? Ah! Michael, Michael, Michael... it's all water under the bridge! What's up with you? Are you scared you're gonna say something and I'll tell you it's the stupidest thing I've ever heard? Haha! Afraid I'll laugh at your movies? Hahaha!"

He awkwardly joins in the laughter, and everything around him starts spinning. At least she's in a good mood. Since running away is no longer an option, he opens his mouth and tries to act smooth.

"Daphné... Daphné, Daphné, Daphné. First off, I just want to say: your talk this afternoon was excellent. Top notch, truly. I was blown away by your reasoning, your style, and your stage presence. I wanted to congratulate you after, but I had dinner plans. Some guys from, uh, the *Journal of Film Studies* who want to do a piece on me. Anyway, it was a bit of a bore. I thought I'd try to catch you after dinner. I wanted to see how you're doing. Looks like I'm in luck! You look truly ravishing."

"The *Journal of Film Studies*? Seriously? Now I've seen it all! Haha! But that's nice of you to say. This afternoon honestly wasn't a big deal. Basically a way of getting a free trip to Hawaii out of the university! Haha! I need another drink. You coming?"

Out the hotel room window, drunken tourists on Waikiki Beach give a resounding whoop at each skyward eruption. A loud brass band moves between the bonfires dotted along the beach, the post-midnight hour briefly forgotten. On TV, a local channel has replaced the usual crackling fireplace on loop with the image of an American flag flapping in the wind. Michael sits on the edge of the bed watching the Stars and Stripes ripple, and it fills him with fortitude.

The bathroom door opens, and Daphné emerges, naked and refreshed. She approaches the bed slowly, her attempt at a sexy slink closer to an unsteady stagger.

"We have some catching up to do, you and I."

Michael exhales, takes a swig from a bottle he stole from the student center, and slips off his boxer shorts. He's Washington. He's Jefferson. He's Lincoln. He's Roosevelt. The bed is Virginia, Texas, the Pacific. Inside and outside the room, there's a celebration of victory, of conquering and conquering again, of ecstasy in the presence of something greater than oneself. From Honolulu to Lac-Mégantic, Corinth to Santa Monica, every step has led here, to this night of promised and forbidden love, to this celebration of transcendence through immanence, to the generation of beauty, to the most absolute act of creation.

"NO, NO, NO! They can't do this to me—not again. I absolutely refuse. We'll continue as planned."

"Listen, Michael, you and I both know how this works. They have too much power. Insubordination isn't an option. Don did his best to make them come around, and look where that..."

The alarmed, questioning look on Michael's face stopped Bruckheimer short.

"What do you mean? What are you trying to say?"

"No, nothing. I'm rambling. Ignore me. It's all the emotions... I think I'm just exhausted."

"Don died of an allergic reaction... didn't he? Is there something I should know?"

"Yes, just as you said, an allergic reaction... Pay no attention to my jabbering. The fact is, we need to change the end of the movie. The studio wants a happy ending, something that makes the audience feel all warm and fuzzy and, ideally, featuring some sort of countdown. I've tried and tried again to make them see your reasoning, but they won't budge: the world as we know it has to be saved."

"But that would undermine the entire film! It's absurd, completely absurd! They're scared, Jerry, that's what it is. They're scared that we're right! They're scared we're going to trigger a wide-scale questioning of reality and, by extension, they're scared of losing their hypnotic power over the masses! We need to free ourselves from those vulgar merchants of discourse and finish the project. Our collective relationship to meaning depends on it."

"It's not that simple, Michael. If we don't go along with what they want, the movie'll never be released. Our work would be doubly in vain. Let's finish it the way they want, even if we have to make a public apology in a few years."

"I don't know, Jerry. I'm tired of giving in. Think of everyone who gave their lives for this shoot. Don't we owe it to them to fight till the end? Look around! Haven't we made enough sacrifices? Doesn't that mean anything to them?"

The place was strikingly inhospitable. Razor-sharp stalagmites jutted up through the unstable ground, and geysers of corrosive gas threatened to erupt at any moment. Thousands of rock fragments drifted through a black sky, backlit by both the Moon and Earth, some of them pelting the surface of the asteroid where survivors of the *Armageddon* shoot had gathered.

Freedom and *Truth* were parked side by side, while the remnants of *Independence* lay upside-down a couple miles further on, near a bottomless chasm. Several hours earlier, to everyone's great surprise, that shuttle's few survivors had found their way back to the group, who'd thought them lost forever. Aboard an all-terrain drilling vehicle that had been stored in the hull of their shuttle, a relieved and euphoric Ben Affleck, Michael Clarke Duncan, and Peter Stormare had appeared at the top of one of the asteroid's peaks, ready to finish the grueling shoot. It had been two days since the forced landing, and the space drilling scenes were delayed due to urgent repairs needed on *Truth*. According to the astronauts, the vessel would soon be in flying order.

"It's not just a decision based on differing philosophical views, Michael. That's part of it, sure, but the studio just learned that *Deep Impact*, which we're up against, will be out a month before us and there's an Earth-asteroid collision in it. They're pulling the rug out from under us. If we don't change the ending, we'll look like plagiarists and that'll be it for us in terms of getting our work out there."

"Are you fucking kidding me?"

"No, I'm afraid I'm completely serious. Listen, son, we don't have much time. Soon our oxygen reserves will be dangerously low. We've got to improvise. We should make the most of the hole we just dug. Let's throw a bomb in it, get off the surface, and blow this whole rock up for real."

"I don't know, Jerry. It's a real atomic bomb. It's dangerous. Plus it's lazy and formulaic from a screenwriting perspective. I'd much rather go with our first idea of a malfunction, where human desire to ensure its permanence is futile when faced with the force of cosmic will."

"I know, so would I. But we need to adapt. If it's any consolation, think of it as our own futile desire to awaken minds when faced with the will of Los Angeles. Let's detonate this bomb, Michael. Listen: Bruce's character could sacrifice himself. There could be a problem and they can't remote detonate the bomb, so he has to stay on the asteroid and blow it up manually. Obviously we can film that scene when we get back. But at least that would be heroic. Lots of fuzzy feelings. That'd placate the studio. Then, we can roll up our sleeves again and come up with another movie. Next time, it'll be the one."

"I don't know... I just don't know... I need a minute alone."

"Yes, of course, take five. But not a minute more. The shuttles are almost ready. We have to act fast. I'll go see Bruce to talk about the changes. Come see me in the cockpit after. And hurry."

Michael walked away from the encampment, head down and hands behind his back, and went to stand at the edge of a cliff. In a brief fit of frustration, he kicked a pointy rock with his boot, sending it flying, free forevermore of the asteroid's low gravitational pull. At his feet, a steep drop ended in a vast field of ice, iron, and silica, and on the horizon, Earth shone for all to see, still euphoric at having narrowly avoided Judgment Day.

From space, Michael could see the United States in a single glance, but this in no way lessened its splendor. "Will I ever make my mark?" he wondered. "Will I ever create something lasting? Will I ever get the chance to express myself, get something on film other than eternal compromise? Or am I no different than that shooting star?"

Michael felt a hand on his shoulder through the thick fabric of his space suit. Dr. Tyson had come over to offer his support during the moment of hopelessness.

"You seem defeated, my friend."

"Professor... I hope this mission has proved of scientific value to you, because the film is going to be a failure."

"I'm sure it's not as bad as all that. No failure is total. In fact, we rarely get the results we set out for. Backward steps are vital in any rigorous process. In science, a hypothesis that's confirmed too easily usual signals dishonest methodology. A true intellectual knows how to build something more solid on the remnants of their ruined projects."

"You have a way with words, Professor. But I don't think I have the strength to keep fighting. I'm tired of being asked to turn my back on the very essence of my projects for political or financial reasons. I dream of making a meaningful film, but am perpetually reduced to creating something sterile."

"Let me guess—they asked you to change the ending?"

"Exactly. I have to give up my innovative vision for something showy and sentimental."

"What are your options, exactly?"

"Bruckheimer suggested we actually blow up the asteroid and superpose it with the father sacrificing himself. It's such an easy out..."

"And do you actually have the technical means to do it?"

"Yes, the technical side isn't a problem. The army loaned us a nuclear warhead. The contract stipulates that we have to bring it back intact, but I'm sure the studio can arrange something... So it's really an artistic problem."

Dr. Tyson paused before replying. He took a moment to contemplate the cosmos.

"Michael, you're being given a chance you won't get again. You should take it. Have you forgotten our last conversation?"

"I'm not sure what you mean."

"You have the chance to create your own big bang. A massive explosion in the heart of interplanetary space. The ultimate act of creation. We don't yet know what will come of it, but according to what science tells us, you could legitimately view this as the start of something new."

Michael's eyes lit up. His thoughts whirled, his head suddenly too small to hold them all. True, he initially wanted his film to be a call to the humility of humankind, but he couldn't simply pass up the chance to play God.

"Thank you, Dr. Tyson. You're right. Now, let's create something."

The modifications to *Truth* were holding up, but the launch was bumpier than expected. Inside the shuttle, the survivors from *Independence* took the seats left vacant by the victims of the crash, while the original co-pilot of *Freedom* took command behind an improvised windshield. Michael, tightly strapped into his seat, ensured the few functional cameras were ready to roll. According to Dr. Tyson's calculations, the shuttles needed to be at least sixty miles from the asteroid to clear the nuclear explosion. In a few moments, Michael could activate the bomb and, he hoped, remake the world a little more in his image.

The seconds scrolled past on one of the screens.

Twenty seconds left. The decimals counted down at a frenetic pace. Despite the g-force pressing him against his seat, Michael managed to turn his head to the left toward Bruckheimer and Dr. Tyson. The two men gripped their armrests, trying to limit the discomfort of the vibrations, but gave him a soothing look, one that said, "Don't be afraid, it's the right thing to do." Just ten seconds to go before the fateful moment. Michael gave them a solemn nod, then focused on the little box, into which was inserted, at the end of a long beaded chain, a big key, and turned it to the right. Three lights turned from red to green.

"Engines!" he yelled into his helmet mic. Five seconds. He took a gloved index finger and lifted the red safety cap to reveal the switch. He exhaled. Looked out the window.

Two.

One.

"Action!"

A few rays of light shine through the fissures of the asteroid, then a dazzling crack splits it along its circumference, as millions of flashes tear through the ether and envelope the asteroid in an ephemeral ring. It ruptures with impossible speed and splinters into two halves that float away from each another in silence, amid a flood of blinding light. Everyone on board shields their eyes, their forearms offering paltry protection. A violent but non-lethal shockwave hits the two shuttles. Michael finds himself half-naked on his hands and knees on a grassy path in the middle of what looks like an orange grove. There's a gentle breeze blowing. The grass is cool and pleasant, and colorful butterflies flit around overly ripe fruit scattered across the ground. An overwhelming feeling of being alone, of having been abandoned, seizes him. He feels a pang of hunger. He tries to stand up, to get help, but his legs are too weak. He loses his balance and falls onto his back. High in the sky, crows caw and circle under the ever-brilliant sun. Terrified, Michael manages to roll onto his stomach and crawl toward the dense enclave of trees in search of shelter. When he reaches the protection of the foliage, he keeps going. He manages to pull himself to his feet from time to time and take a few wobbly steps between the tree trunks, but otherwise he covers the distance mostly on his hands and knees. The farther he gets, the stronger the pull of a voice that sounds far away at first, then closer and closer. It is the only thing guiding him amid the mass of identical trees. The orange trees ahead are sparser. He reaches the edge of the orchard, exhausted. There, wearing a white toga, his back to Michael, an elderly man addresses a group of mostly enrapt young boys. The scene has a troubling effect on Michael: he is certain the preacher is his father. He tries calling to him to get his attention, but realizes in frustration that he does not yet possess the gift of speech. Meaningless cries escape his mouth. Neither his father nor the group reacts. He insists, redoubling his efforts. He tries to call out, "Papa!" but nothing but a jumble of syllables comes out. "Baampas! Bammp...aas!" he shouts. His efforts finally appear to bear fruit. His father, still speaking to his students, cocks his head slightly to the side, his ear toward Michael. "Baaampas!"

The man reaches discreetly behind his lower back with his right hand, then flicks his wrist, as though swatting away an unwelcome insect. Baby Michael sits dumfounded for a moment, shocked by his father's reaction, at being refused the attention he demands. He continues on, crawling toward the group, determined to claim his right as son, but a woman's hands grab hold of him and yank him backward, under the trees and out of sight. He shrieks. The words his mother whispers to him are confusing, abstruse. He wants to see her face but he can't. Why isn't she speaking to him in English? Why won't she let him see his father? All of a sudden, everything becomes clear. Her words sting Michael to the very core as the clouds lift from his mother's ramblings like a revelation: "They mustn't see you," she repeats through sobs.

A strident alarm pulls Michael from his reverie. His soaking wet space suit clings to his skin. A crew member is trying to put out a fire with an extinguisher. Seeing Michael's distressed gaze, Bruckheimer and Dr. Tyson wave their arms in his direction. The alarm stops. *Truth* stabilizes, then prepares for its descent to Earth.

Resentment. That's the feeling pumping through Michael's veins, now that he is back to himself. Resentment, but also shame. Shame at the way he treated Jim and Harriett, at the way he must have broken their hearts, at the ungrateful way he acted. For so long, he's believed that deciphering the mystery of his origin would bring relief, but he feels none. There are still shadowy areas, but one thing is now clear: the fact he was adopted means his birth parents abandoned him, that they didn't want him. Worse still, they were ashamed of him. They considered him a nuisance. Jim and Harriett may have lied to him, but they only ever meant to protect him. Not once did they ignore him, not once did they deprive him of love, not once did they make him feel he didn't measure up.

"I have some apologizing to do," he says to himself.

ON MORNINGS AFTER

A WARM LIGHT FILTERS through the sheer hotel curtains, waking Michael from his slumber. Despite his dry
mouth, ringing head, and churning stomach, he feels
happy. Light. Victorious.

Lying on his back, eyes half-open, Michael turns his
head slowly to find he's alone in the bed. His eyelids
flutter as he fully wakes. Then comes a niggling doubt.
A twinge of nausea. He examines the vacant spot to
his right more carefully. The sheets are rumpled, still
warm to the touch. His brain feels sluggish. The muffled sound of a plastic bottle hitting the shower floor
confirms it wasn't all a dream. He can hear the sound of
running water on the other side of the bathroom door.
He inhales deeply, exhales slowly.

He sits up and pauses for a moment at the edge of
the bed. An evening of sex has not completely nullified
the after-effects of the alcohol. The pasty feeling in
his mouth makes him feel sick. He manages to stand,
stretches, and walks to the window. Bracing himself for

the inevitable shock, as if he were about to jump into a pool of icy water, he pulls the curtains wide open, at once blinded by the light. As the brightness fades, he drinks in the beauty of the day. Fluffy clouds are scattered across the calm, clear blue sky. The whole of Hawaii seems to still be asleep on this radiant fourth of July. From the sixth floor of the hotel he can see Ford Island, the military base floating in the middle of Pearl Harbor. Mock battleships surround the island, positioned exactly as the USS *Arizona*, USS *Oklahoma*, USS *West Virginia*, USS *California*, USS *Nevada*, USS *Tennessee*, and USS *Maryland* had been on the morning of December 7, 1941. Except for a few keen technicians, the set is deserted, ready for production's most important day of shooting; the following day at dawn, the entire crew will gather to film the fateful bombing scene. The real and financial stakes are high. The slightest error in execution and everything will have to be redone, at great cost. The surprise attack had been meticulously choreographed over the last few days. The Japanese government had loaned them some vintage airplanes in exchange for a few million and the promise of a flattering and nuanced depiction of its army. Never had the special effects team, who'd been with Michael since his first film, had such an enormous task before them. More than fifty tons of C4 had been attached to the hulls of the mock warships, ready to explode in sequence and give the macabre aerial ballet its raison d'être. The actors and extras have all sworn to deliver an impeccable performance, lest they kiss their Hollywood futures goodbye. Despite the risks, Michael, the most devoted of kamikazes, feels surprisingly Zen.

The street outside the hotel is empty save the odd delivery vehicle. A town clock reads ten thirty, but with the streets so quiet, it feels closer to six in the morning. A dazzling reflection momentarily blinds Michael, who looks away then back again, trying to find its source. Across the street behind a palm tree, a man, no doubt the same who'd followed him the previous evening, points a camera in his direction. Surprisingly, Michael no longer feels hostile, just indifferent. He smiles and nonchalantly waves his right hand, unconcerned by his nakedness being offered up on a platter for the tabloids.

Michael leaves the curtains open and goes back to sit down on the edge of the bed. He looks down at his penis and murmurs, "Not bad, eh? Frankly, it was better than anything we've had before... More natural, I'd say... I think we've got a little soul searching to do, you and I. It seems we were wrong about love... Shall we set the record straight?"

Behind the bathroom door, the shower has stopped. The sound of running water is replaced by Daphné's voice, not quite loud enough to be addressing Michael. She must be on the phone. He tries to make out what she's saying, but her voice is muffled, the words indistinct through the wall. Then the conversation ends, and Michael readies himself for his lover. He lies down on his side, facing the bathroom door, one knee casually

229

bent. His mind is filled with images of the previous night and his member slowly stiffens, ready for the next round. After a few minutes of silence, he hears the doorknob turn.

Daphné appears, dressed and made up, ready for the day. She recoils slightly at the sight of Michael lying there with a suggestive grin.

"You're still here? You have to leave. My husband just got to the airport, and he's on his way to the hotel."

Her words send a shockwave through Michael and leave him breathless. There's a ringing in his ears. He feels faint, but pulls himself together and instinctively turns to the window, certain someone has accidentally detonated one of the C4 charges on set. To his surprise, the bay is calm, no fireballs in sight. The ships are intact. But his body still reacts as though there's been an explosion, his skin covered in goosebumps. He turns to Daphné, confused.

"Wh... Sorry, I could've sworn that... What did you say?"

"My husband. He's on his way. He can't know about this. You have to leave. Plus, I have work to do. I applied for a big grant and a lot of the committee members are in town—I've got some buttering up to do."

"Your husband? You mean... you're married?"

"Yes, Michael. That's what that means. You really are a genius."

"But... I don't understand! We're back together now! You can't be married!"

"Honestly, Michael, don't be ridiculous. We slept together, yes, but don't get carried away. The way you're reacting just confirms it was a mistake."

"A mistake? No, Daphné! It wasn't a mistake! It's the natural order of things! You and I are made for each other! We both know that! It's your marriage that's the mistake! The proof is that you just slept with me. If you really loved your husband, you never would have betrayed him like this!"

"Let's get a couple things clear. First, we're never getting back 'together.' Get that into your head. We live in completely different worlds. Sure, for a couple of months we thought it could work, but that was delusional, a misunderstanding—that's all. Second, I didn't really betray Danny. Of course I'd rather he never found out about last night because it'll complicate things unnecessarily, but I don't consider myself guilty of anything. You owed me that sex, Michael. You owed it to me, and all I did was take what I was due. Now that's all out of the way, we can both finally move on. Last night wasn't a new beginning. It was the end of the story—or more like the epilogue. Now get your clothes on and go back to your teen-boy movies."

Daphné picks up Michael's crumpled clothes and throws them on the bed. Michael stares, his eyes wide and vacant, as though he's somewhere else. Daphné claps her hands a few times to get him to snap out of it.

"You don't have to say anything, but if you want to ponder your life choices, do it somewhere else."

231

"So who is this... Danny?"

"It doesn't matter, Michael."

"I'm going, Daphné. I'll leave you alone. I just want to know. Please. I want to know what makes him so special. I want to know what it would've taken for you to choose me."

Daphné frowns and closes her eyes, sighing. "We work together. He's a tenured film studies professor at UCLA. A truly brilliant man with a well-paved career path. I honestly believe he's going to change the field—he has everything it takes to make it big. His name is Danny Walker, if you must know."

Michael's heart begins to race. He suddenly finds it hard to breathe, as though his lungs are filling with water. Try as he might to concentrate on the present, all he can see are images—ones he had often pictured during preproduction, but now coming to him in staggering clarity—of torpedoes hitting the USS *Arizona*. More than ever, he feels empathy for the sunken battleships. More than ever, just as he's getting to the bottom of things, he is speechless at the thought of filming Cuba Gooding Jr. sinking in flames in the middle of the Oahu waters.

"Danny Walker? From Tennessee? Who studied at Wesleyan?"

"Yes... You know him? I guess you've read his articles? Or his books?"

"No, Daphné, NO! You can't do this to me! Not Danny! Danny was like a brother to me!"

"A brother? What are you talking about?"

232

"We studied together. We were college roommates for four years. We lost touch a long time ago, but that doesn't matter. He's still the closest thing I've ever had to a best friend. You can't be with him!"

"Listen, Michael, best friend or not, you have to understand that I've moved on. You were dead to me after *Bad Boys*. Granted this is all a bit weird, and a pretty unfortunate situation, but I couldn't have known. He's never once spoken about you. Anyway, it doesn't change anything. What I have with Danny is infinitely better than what we ever could have had together. With Danny, what you see is what you get, as you Americans love to say. No surprises—except good ones. And frankly, I have a hard time believing you and Danny were ever all that close. He's an accomplished intellectual. You're like a prepubescent teen who wants people to believe he's an accomplished intellectual. And frankly, you haven't convinced all that many people... Are you going to get dressed or what?"

Michael instantly drops to the floor, sure that a squadron of fighter jets is spraying the front of the hotel with bullets. He glances out the window: the sky is perfectly serene. Perplexed, he stands back up and puts his pants on.

"God you're weird. I certainly dodged a bullet with you."

"With all due respect, I *am* an intellectual. My films are proof of that. I'm just misunderstood. I'm ahead of my time."

"Ha! The great genius, misunderstood by his peers! Now I've heard it all!"

"Don't mock me, Daphné. You've already hurt me enough. I'm serious. My films are essays on serious and complex topics. *Bad Boys* is a film on decolonization, regardless of what you insist on believing. *The Rock*, as a matter of fact, is about that very lack of understanding by one's peers. *Armageddon* is about a post-human future that's better at decoding the mystery of meaning. And *Pearl Harbor*, my latest film, is both a tribute to my country's history and a reflection on the freedoms an artist enjoys when fictionalizing reality. From the moment I choose to create a work of fiction based not only on real events, but also on real people like Roosevelt, what's permissible? What's not? If I change what really happened for aesthetic reasons, am I a liar or a creator? Is what I'm doing defamation? Where exactly is the line? It's a rich subject, one that resonates with me unlike anything before!"

Daphné rolls her eyes and massages her temples. "Fuck, Michael, you're so intense. You're giving me a headache. Look, maybe you think your movies say something, but honestly, it just doesn't come across when you watch them."

"You mean you've seen my films?"

"Of course. I've seen all of them. I was curious, that's all. But I felt the same way every single time: they're just empty shells. And there are so many problems with them—it's excruciating! Your characters, for instance, are always one-dimensional. It doesn't feel like they're real people, just clumsy pretexts for a bunch of action scenes."

"Poor soldiers," thinks Michael, only half listening. "They were in over their heads. All those fighter planes... the bombs... bullets flying all around them... ships breaking apart under their feet... Truly tragic. What chance did they have, pistols against warplanes? How could they have anticipated an attack of such magnitude, such devastation? Above all, how had the nation managed to survive—how had it managed to stay on its feet? A foreign power had pierced the heart of America, but the American citizens, despite the Hawaiian defeat, showed resilience. How? Perhaps because they knew they were right. They knew humanity's salvation rested on their shoulders."

"You say that," Michael starts up again after a moment, "because you weren't in the right state of mind for *Bad Boys*. It was all those journalists hounding you. All that stress. It triggered a kind of irrational hostility in you, and ever since, it's that association you make when you sit down to watch one of my films. It immediately returns you to that unreceptive state. It's like a sort of trauma. But there are ways to get past it. If we just talk about it a bit more, I'm sure you'll have faith in me again. You'll be able to appreciate the rich, complex discourse of my films."

"Look, maybe it's clear in your head, but you can't execute for shit, Michael. It's just confusing a lot of the time, like you're trying too hard. The in-your-face aspect of your movies, the constant stylistic turns, the heaviness, it's all just to hide the fact that there's zero plot. And you need to stop telling yourself stories. I don't give a shit about journalists. It was unpleasant, but what happened at that premiere has nothing to do with how I view your work. I didn't like it because you promised me a film on decolonization, an intellectually rigorous film, and what I got, in the end, as I already told you, was a trigger-happy movie for teens."

"I... No, I think you're missing the point. Sure, my films haven't always lived up to their potential, but that's because of the studios. They've often forced me to dilute the content. They've stopped me from expressing myself freely. I'm a victim of censorship, Daphné."

"You're being a bit dramatic, Michael. I think it's all in your head. That's my honest opinion."

"It's not! You don't understand me, Daphné. How can you be so smart but so blind? All it would take is for someone, someone like you, to study my work in an academic context for everyone to start taking me seriously, for people to genuinely dissect my work."

"What the hell do you care about academic recognition? The general public loves what you do! They're rushing the doors to see you blow stuff up. And you're rich because of it! Isn't that enough?"

"The public is fickle. They watch the film, then they move on to the next thing. But institutional approval would give me a place in the ranks of history, long after my death. I'm not asking for much, really. I just want to be recognized for my intelligence. And I want to be immortal."

"Ha! The only chance of you being studied in college is if one of the boys your movies are aimed at grows up to be a decent intellectual and decides to write a book that restores your image in the eyes of the elite. And that's wishful thinking! Now, for the last time: get the hell out, or I'm calling security."

Michael looks at Daphné—no doubt for the last time—knowing he has to leave.

"I would have loved you," he says, and closes the door behind him.

ON CONFUSION

"ONE MORE THEN I'M OUT. I'm only doing it because I'm under contract."

Michael knocks back a glass of ouzo and slams it down on the vaguely sticky surface of the bar. The barman comes over and pours him another double, which he knocks back with a grimace.

"I think he'll take a break," says Bruckheimer to the barman.

The bar is somewhat dingy and nearly deserted, save a few regulars whose grim expectations for life are reflected in their rough, neglected appearance. The USA demolition derby plays on the only working TV in the place, sheet metal crumpling in silence. Behind the bar, a neon Budweiser sign flickers half-heartedly, emitting an ominous electrical crackle every now and then.

"A failure. That's what I am. I've got to be honest with myself. I'm just a joke, a bad joke that's run its course. I'm telling you: after *Bad Boys 2*, I'm out. You'll have to find yourself a new recruit."

"The alcohol is clouding your thoughts, Michael. We still have a lot of work ahead of us. *Pearl Harbor* wasn't our best work, I admit. But I still have much to teach you. Things that Don himself taught me."

Bruckheimer tenderly places his hand over Michael's, which rests limply on the bar. Michael pulls away, pouting, then scratches his chest and his chin, where a few hairs have started to sprout. A sorrowful, almost lovesick look flashes across Bruckheimer's face.

"I'm done, and I'm going to find a new woman. Someone who understands me. Someone who can help me stop seeing Daphné's face every time I close my eyes."

"A woman? Have you learned nothing? Women are a disappointment and a waste of time. You shouldn't squander your potential obsessing over how to please them."

"I don't know, Jerry. To be honest, I've just about had enough of your advice. It's always the same story, and look where it's gotten me. The love of my life despises me. And academics and journalists have nothing but disdain for me."

"Opinion is something intermediary between knowledge and ignorance."

"Enough with the proverbs! Even my parents abandoned me! If you're as good a mentor as you say, you'd have told me to patch things up with them long ago. But no! It's like you want me all to yourself... And now it's too late. They've vanished! Disappeared without a trace!"

"Michael, you know I've done everything in my power to help you find them. You're treating me like this because you're confused and upset."

"Lies!" Michael shouts, hurling his empty glass at the TV. "If you'd really wanted to help, you'd have found them! You'd have gotten answers from the fraternity that bought my childhood home to use for their orgies or keg parties or who knows what! You'd have convinced the police to keep looking! You wouldn't have settled for not knowing! It's like you don't want the mystery to be solved!"

"For heaven's sake, Michael, calm down! You know as well as I do that we did everything possible to find them. But they didn't leave a trace. Not a single trace. It's almost as if they never existed."

Everything around Michael begins to spin, as though he's stuck inside an escape pod in high seas. Momentarily dazed, he tries to fight the spasms contracting his stomach. He closes his eyes and concentrates on his breathing. The room stops moving. He finally manages to calm himself.

"Do you really think they're in witness protection?" asks Michael, stifling an anise-flavored belch.

"It seems to be the only feasible explanation. In the wrong place at the wrong time. Witnesses to something they shouldn't have seen. Then relocated by the FBI and given new identities. In Kansas or Idaho or who knows where. It would explain why there's no trace of them. I honestly don't see another reasonable hypothesis."

Michael stares into space. On the TV, a Camaro flips over and bursts into flames.

"I'm such a fool. I broke their hearts. I'm so selfish. And now I've missed my only chance to pick up the pieces. For the rest of their lives they'll think I loathe them, when the only loathsome one in the story is me. They'll never know how much I love them."

"Don't be so hard on yourself, Michael. Perhaps their absence, just like that of the young woman you were so taken with, is crucial to the intensity of your affection. Don't forget: what we did not, what is not, what is missing, these are objects of love."

"Pfft... If that's true, then I can see why I love philosophers so much. Because I'm incapable of being one! It's so pathetic... I've spent my whole life trying to understand, but the closer I get, the less I understand! Meaning is like cornstarch mixed with water: as soon as I think I've got it in my grasp, it seeps through my fingers!"

Bruckheimer leans back slightly. For a moment he seems elsewhere, lost in thought, then he returns to the present and soulfully contemplates his protégé. Slowly he rises from his barstool.

"I'm going to the bathroom."

Bruckheimer walks away from the bar as Michael turns, scowls at his back and gives him the finger. Then he reaches into his pocket and casually tosses a few hundred dollar bills over the bar.

"Give me the bottle."

Michael takes a long swig from the bottle. Ouzo running down his cheeks, he stands up and trips, but catches himself on a table just in time. He staggers toward the door, anxious to leave before Bruckheimer comes back. Outside, the oppressive Los Angeles heat hits him like a wave, and beads of sweat instantly form on his back and face. The dizziness returns, even stronger. There's only booze to cool him down. His balance deserting him by the minute, he wanders aimlessly down the sidewalk and stops abruptly after a couple dozen steps. On the other side of the street, a tabloid photographer is checking his last few shots on his camera screen. Michael gives him a hard, defiant stare then, as though he isn't sure what else to do, he scowls and gives him the middle finger. The photographer ignores him. Michael is confused, then insulted, then feels the urgent need to urinate. He surrenders to the urge, undoing his belt and relieving himself not against a wall but directly into the street, in full view of several outraged passersby, their indignant comments alerting the attention of the photographer, who finally casts a disinterested glance in his direction, rolls his eyes, then goes back to what he was doing. Pants around his ankles, Michael feels the blood rush to his head. Before his bladder has finished emptying, he starts crossing the street to confront the photographer, but stumbles helplessly and falls face-first into a puddle of his own piss pooling around him. The shock and reek of ammonia is too much for Michael's already sensitive stomach. Like a whale washed up on the beach and blown to pieces, Michael, bare-assed and flat on the ground, spews a shower of acrid, lump-filled vomit into the air, some of which remains clinging to his lips. A few of the pedestrians who've been watching on in shock or amusement now make the sign of the cross.

Drunk as he is, Michael is well aware of the pathetic scene he's making. He struggles to get up, his hands sunk in his own spatter, and cries out with a force that startles even him.

"Hey you! Paparazzi guy! I'm Michael Bay! Michael Bay! I did *Pearl Harbor*! I did.... I did *Armageddon*! Take some pictures—come on! Sell them! Write whatever you want! Tell everyone I'm just a has-been! Tell 'em my girlfriend left me and I'm drinking like a loser to try to relive the one time I ever slept with a woman! Hey, you! Paparazzi guy! Go ahead! Take some pictures! I'm Michael Bay!"

"Shut up!" the photographer finally shoots back. "I don't care!"

"But... but... I did, uh, *Bad Boys*! With Will Smith!"

"Yeah, I know who you are. But I don't care. You're not worth a dime."

"What do you mean not worth a dime? I'm a money-making machine!"

"Great, good for you. But no one's going to waste their time on you. You're so... 1996."

"What are you talking about? There's always photographers following me around!"

243

"Well, bro, then you've got a problem, because I guarantee that any self-respecting photographer stopped paying attention to you at least five years ago. Now do yourself a favor and go home, or go drive your car into a tree."

Frowning, Michael opens his mouth to say something but for once he can't find the words. He tries to understand the situation, struggles to gather his intellectual faculties, but he can't seem to organize the information coherently. Just then, a panicked Bruckheimer runs up behind him.

"Michael! Michael, what are you doing? What's come over you? What is this spectacle? Put your clothes on!"

Bruckheimer helps Michael to his feet and pulls up his pants. Michael doesn't resist, too busy trying to process it all. The crowd disperses, having had its fun.

"What's going on, Michael? You're not yourself. Come on, I'll bring you home. I'll make you some coffee. You can have my bed."

"They don't care about me anymore..." mumbles Michael, more to himself than anything.

"Who? The paparazzi? That's good news! You've said it yourself: they're a nuisance."

"They aren't the paparazzi, those..."

"You need rest, Michael. Come with me. I'll look after you."

Michael turns to Bruckheimer suspiciously, and shakes his shoulders free of the producer's hold.

"Leave me alone. I can't think clearly when you're around," he says, his sentences punctuated by loud hiccups.

"You're confused, my son. The alcohol is preventing you from thinking straight. I only want to help."

"More bullshit! You want to help? So tell me: if they aren't paparazzi, then who are the photographers who've been following me for years?"

"You're paranoid, Michael. No one is following you. So maybe a few people took your photo without asking, but that's just how it is in Hollywood. It comes with the job."

"Fans? Tourists? That's your explanation? So, tell me, why is that admirer over there with a camera hiding behind that mailbox?"

Michael jerks his head toward a mailbox a few hundred feet away, behind which a young man crouches, camera pressed up against his face. The photographer Michael had just been speaking to is already long gone, off in search of new starlets to disgrace. Bruckheimer squints over at the mailbox and tries to make out the bent-over silhouette blending into the black of the night.

"Where? I can't see anything."

"Don't play dumb. Over there, across the street behind that mailbox."

"Oh, yes, OK, you're right. I wouldn't worry about it. He's probably just some timid fan who doesn't want to disturb you with his display of voyeurism. In fact, I would say he's more respectful than most tourists! Come, let's go over and congratulate him on his civic-mindedness."

Bruckheimer waves a hand in the air, but Michael jumps on him straight away and forces his arm down. Aware he's been spotted, the photographer calmly stands up and, without waving back, walks to the next corner, turns right, and disappears.

"Now look what you've done! He's getting away thanks to you!"

"I was only trying to be nice. He was probably embarrassed. Alright... let's find a taxi and grab that coffee."

"No, not me. I'm going to follow him."

"Don't be childish, Michael."

With a surprisingly strong grip, Bruckheimer seizes Michael by the shoulders. Infuriated, Michael breaks away and pushes him violently, sending him falling back into the pool of vomit and urine.

"I said leave me alone!"

Still drunk on ouzo, too impatient to wait for a passing taxi, Michael starts running after the photographer. He'd once read in a scientific journal that physical activity was the best way to sober up quickly; tonight he will put a theory to the test, just as he'd always loved doing in his youth. Behind him, a defeated Bruckheimer lies on the ground, watching his protégé speed away. Just before Michael disappears from sight, he cries, "Michael! Stop! You're not ready!" Then under his breath, "Or are you?"

The effects of the alcohol start to wear off and Michael, who hasn't run this far since his college triathlon days, pushes through the pain and shortness of breath. Every ounce of strength drains from his legs but, like a bobble-head in perpetual motion, they keep moving by themselves, propelled solely by inertia. His hair and clothing drenched, heart pounding in his ears, body filled with carbon dioxide, Michael only just manages to keep his target's car in sight, once again determined to get answers to his questions. Los Angeles neighborhoods push by under his feet one after the next, from the most affluent to the most notorious. Enormous, painful blisters form on his heels, and the combination of exercise-induced dehydration and alcohol turns into an irritating headache.

Michael tries to save energy by emptying his mind, thinking of nothing, but as usual he is unable to do so. "Who are you? What do you want from me? Why is Jerry acting like this? What will I do after my films? Work with my hands? Build something? Why can't I make them respect me? Should I have just continued my doctoral studies? Will I find love one day? Could Jim and Harriett have forgiven me? Why was I so selfish? Does Danny know Daphné and I were in love? Why wasn't I ever able to ask her to marry me? Would it have changed anything? What kind of car should I buy next? Why is it only teenage boys like my films? Why is meaning constantly changing? Where the hell is this guy going anyway?"

Michael's heart races faster, something he thought impossible under the circumstances, as he watches the car he's following take Burbank Boulevard and cross the boundary separating Woodland Hills and Hidden Hills. These are the hills he had once ridden up and down tirelessly on his mountain bike, but had visited only once in the last twenty years when, newly returned from space and finally ready to patch things up with Jim and Harriett, he had discovered his childhood home abandoned by his parents and taken over by frat boys in togas, oversized Greek letters now hanging above the door.

Other than the modern and impressively large white house's new vocation, almost nothing has changed in the small middle-class suburb. The trees have grown, further isolating the place from the outside world, but also giving it a more mature, noble, distinguished look. The car slows and continues down increasingly familiar roads until it finally turns onto the street where Michael grew up. His feet slow involuntarily, a physical manifestation of the denial that is now taking over. He falls to the ground, exhausted, his knees hitting the gravel, but keeps his eyes on the car, its taillights giving off a red glow once it pulls up in front of the white house. The car comes to a complete stop, and an enormous wrought iron gate opens to let it in.

Panting and confused, Michael hobbles over to the gate. Through the bars, he can see the man he was trailing walk into what was once his home. Dawn is approaching, and Michael realizes he's not currently equipped to take effective action. He decides to go home, sleep for a few hours, eat at least two full meals, come up with a plan, and return at nightfall to show these new tenants the price you pay when you fuck with Michael Bay.

THE DAY'S LAST RAYS dissipate as the sky fades from orange to lunar blue. Dressed in black, his face masked in a balaclava and a pair of night-vision goggles on his head, Michael crouches inside a hedge, away from prying eyes, and goes over his plan of attack. He's got his Kevlar vest on, as a precaution. The gym bag over his shoulder contains various tools intended to help in the successful completion of his mission: a few stun grenades, a grappling hook with sixty feet of rope, a tranquilizer-dart gun, a remote-control car, a small military shovel, a rag soaked in chloroform, a Taser, and, in case of emergency, some plastic explosives.

A high fence surrounds the modern and impressively large white house and its property. Behind it, Michael can see four watchmen in togas, all bearing the same lightning tattoo. The guards alternate posts like clockwork. Once he's sure the road is deserted, Michael silently breaks ground with his shovel and begins digging out enough earth so he can slip, like a wild animal, under the fence. When one of the guards nears his point of entry, Michael freezes, belly to the grass, stops breathing, then keeps digging until the next sweep. After ten minutes of excavation the hole appears big enough to fit through. Despite his impressive agility, Michael realizes there won't be time to crawl under the fence undetected: he'll need a diversion.

From his bag, Michael pulls out a remote-control car—a miniature replica of a shiny Dodge Viper—and its controller. He maneuvers the two levers, and the mini car reacts by heading first to the opposite end of the wall, then, when the time comes, gliding between two iron bars and entering the grounds in full view of one of the guards. He stops patrolling, suspicious, then approaches it with apparent amusement. He looks around for a young boy in distress, but in vain. Michael, still out of sight, observes the scene from afar. He can't quite make out what they're saying but gathers the guard has called another man over, who leaves his post to give him a hand. The strategy has been more successful than he hoped: not only is the path clear, but Michael has more room to maneuver now that the two men are focused entirely on the object at hand, swerving out of their reach. They appear to be deep in conversation. Michael silently lowers his infrared glasses, slides his bag under the fence, and slips illegally onto the property of the house he grew up in.

As he approaches the building, a third guard suddenly appears, rounding the corner from behind the house. The two men come face to face, look each other up and down in silence like two duelists, each waiting for the other to make the slightest move. But Michael has a distinct visual advantage. Through the dark, he can see every detail of the guard's face glowing in various hues of bright green. The man reminds him of the Coconut Grove Club kidnappers. His eyes are mysterious, reflecting the light like a raccoon in the black of night. He smiles strangely when he sees Michael, then the other two guards, still transfixed by the little car, call the man's name—Anatole. Michael takes advantage of the distraction to whip out his gun and shoot the man in the neck with a sleep dart, sending him deep into an instant slumber.

Familiar with the property's layout, Michael quickly finds a hedge, where he stashes the limp body, then heaves the grappling hook up onto the roof and manages to pull himself up just as the fourth guard appears unsuspectingly beneath his feet.

High up beneath the starry sky, Michael has a stunning view of the playground of his childhood. He is hit with a wave of nostalgia and stops for a moment to take in his familiar surroundings. He lowers the binocular lens on his goggles and notes that, other than a new tree in the middle of the yard, the place is just as he remembers. Except for one detail that fills him with raw emotion: the grass is still somewhat patchy where his electric train exploded some thirty years ago. It would have been easy to lay down a few rolls of sod—strange not to, even—in the spot where it had been torn apart, but nothing had been done. In fact, the area is now cordoned off by a decorative fence that appears to protect it and highlight its importance. Neither Jim nor Harriett nor the new occupants had wished to remove its trace.

Michael takes his knife and cuts through the waterproof seal around the skylight in the second-floor washroom. He carefully removes the Plexiglas dome and silently drops down into the shower, where he waits for a minute. All is quiet. An impressive stack of books sits next to the toilet, and a generic Greek-isle landscape hangs on the wall. A small bowl of bergamot-scented potpourri rests on the counter near the sink, along with a razor, shaving cream, and a tube of lubricant. The sound of footsteps gets louder outside the door. Michael presses himself into a corner of the shower, against the tiles and out of sight. The hinges of the bathroom door creak and he's blinded by the light as it's amplified through his glasses, which he removes carefully and quietly. Someone else is in the room. Michael is hyper aware of himself. The strap of his bag is peeking out of the shower door. He hears the tap turn on, then water rushing. A cloud of steam gradually fills the room. The noise of the water gives him leeway to move a bit. He crouches down and pulls from his bag a dentist's mirror, which he uses to assess the scene: a boy of about sixteen has his toga up around his waist and is meticulously shaving his pubic region. It's the perfect time to act. In one swift movement, Michael slips behind him and covers his mouth and nose with the chloroform-soaked rag. Then he hides the limp body, in the shower this time.

The second-floor hallway is deserted. To the left, his parents' former bedroom. To the right, at the end of the hall, his old room. Crouching, Michael makes his way along the darkened hall of his childhood, the dart gun gripped between his palms following his every glance. Michael is instinctively drawn to his room and heads in its direction, opening every door along the way with the nose of his pistol. What used to be Jim's office, Harriett's darkroom, his playroom, and the family library are now a projection room, sauna, conference room, and small gym. All the doors are ajar but his. He can hear footsteps downstairs, but no one else has come up. Michael checks that he's still alone, grabs the door handle with his left hand, and slowly turns it: it's unlocked. His heart hammers in his temples. He closes his eyes, inhales, exhales, inhales, exhales, opens his eyes, and pushes open the door to find a pitch-black room. Rather than activate his military equipment, he flicks the wall switch and closes the door behind him.

A storage room. That's what it looks like. That's what this room, so fundamental in developing his capacity for critical thinking, has been reduced to. Stacks and stacks of cardboard boxes now fill the space. He knows it's irrational, but he can't help feeling irritated at the lack of respect the new occupants have for his past. An old 8mm projector is collecting dust between two boxes. The only piece of furniture is a desk against the opposite wall, near the window he so often gazed through, searching in vain for the constellations visible in the skies above rural Orange County. Above the desk, half hidden by one of the many stacks of boxes, a bulletin board covered in photos catches his eye. He clears a path through the archives, fearing the worst. What he sees leaves him lightheaded, and he loses his balance for a moment: the pictures are all of him, confirming his suspicions. A dozen snapshots tacked to the board provide a startlingly accurate summary of the past few weeks, from trips to the market and research sessions at the library to meditative strolls through the streets of Los Angeles and his humiliating altercation with the uninterested tabloid photographer. In the top left corner, a headshot of Daphné has a giant X in permanent marker through it. On the desk, a detailed schedule of his daily activities is divided into shifts, each task associated, in a separate column, with a handwritten name and signature: Constantine, Agrippa, Hermes, or Theophane.

Michael is mesmerized. He feels his usual acuity slipping away, as if into quicksand. Out of the corner of his eye, he sees that each box is marked with a month and year. He puts his gun down on the table and opens one of them. Inside, files full of carefully organized pictures, notes, and reports—the detailed archives of his entire life, from Fireball Sunday to the present day. Increasingly furious, he tears open the boxes and empties their contents onto the floor, stunned at the sight of certain documents: a contract with Dr. Tyson stapled to a text that appears to be a transcription of their conversation aboard *Truth*, restaurant receipts clipped to photos of Daphné and Danny, receipts for gifts purchased for Jeanine Basinger, a copy of the Apollo gym lease, compromising photos of Detective Hummel... Michael falters, nauseous and breathless, and falls to the floor as dozens of pages zigzag down around him. All he can think is: *câlisse*.

The door opens and a man appears in the doorway. At first, he doesn't notice the light is already on, distracted by the camera in his hand. Then he sees Michael lying on the ground in a pile of papers. Michael stares back with bloodshot eyes. He recognizes the man. It's the photographer he pushed up against a wall at Don Simpson's funeral.

"Michael..." the photographer says softly, with a strange smile.

Then he shoves over a pile of boxes and whirls to go get help. He rushes toward the hall, but trips and hits his head on the parquet floor, his right leg caught in Michael's grappling hook. Michael launches himself in anger at the photographer, grabs him by the feet, pulls him into the middle of the room, and shuts the door. He flips the man onto his back, sits on his legs to immobilize him, then punches him in the face.

"Who are you?!" Punch.

"Who are you? Why are you following me? What's going on here?"

"Is it ever possible to know what's really going on?"

Another punch. The photographer spits out a tooth and a mouthful of blood. An oniony smell drifts up toward Michael.

"Enough with all the mystery! I want a straight answer! Who are you working for? Why are you documenting my life?"

"Michael... don't kid yourself! You love mysteries. An unexamined life is not worth living."

Michael raises his fist, ready to smash in the man's face with the power and ease of an asteroid. He stops, lowers his arm, and relaxes his knuckles. But instead of giving the photographer a moment of respite, he reaches for the Taser inside his bag.

"You *will* answer me."

Michael presses the Taser against the ribs of the photographer, who starts convulsing, his eyes rolling back in his head.

"Why me? What did I ever do to you?"

"We... we only want what's best for you, Michael."

"What's best for me? What's BEST for ME??"

Michael holds the Taser up against the man's head and fires off an electric shock. Foam froths from the corners of his mouth. His body goes limp. Michael stands up, blood simmering. A terrifying "FUCK!" echoes through the house. Screw a covert approach. He grabs his bag, reloads his gun, and kicks the door open. On the main floor, a dozen people are congregating, getting themselves organized, yelling orders to each other in a language Michael now realizes is Greek. He strides toward the spiral staircase, pulls the pins out of two grenades, and chucks them down the steps. The two blasts go off nearly simultaneously, disorienting the momentarily blinded enemy troops. Michael seizes his chance, sliding down the railing to the foyer, shooting darts as he goes, four of which hit their mark. Michael jumps down and kicks in the kneecap of a young man standing at the foot of the banister. He screams as his leg snaps backward. The men still standing slowly begin to recover from the blasts. Michael notices that none of them are armed, but continues his takedowns with the same determination. One of his targets gets up and takes off toward a phone on the wall, just as the most athletic of the group rushes angrily at Michael. With nowhere to run, Michael first points his gun at the boy running to call for help, pulls the trigger, and watches as the dart misses his jugular and lodges itself in his left eye, eliciting a scream that soon fades under the dart's tranquilizing effects. Michael tries to dodge the giant who's still rushing toward him, but he's too slow. The boy throws his full weight at him, knocking Michael's gun out of his hand and making him see stars. Shaken and unable to stand, Michael feels himself pulled up by his jacket and dragged into the hall. An enormous designer chandelier that his mother had shipped from Europe shimmers overhead. He finds himself in the middle of a wide circular pattern in the floor tiles, face to face with the giant, who's let him go and is now rotating his shoulders as he looks Michael up and down. The two boys who are still unscathed bolt away to the right, toward what used to be the Bay family's home theater.

Michael and his opponent circle each other in an invisible ring, shifting back and forth in fight stance. Arms out in front and hands almost touching, they study each other. The teenager attacks first. He leaps at Michael and easily wraps his powerful arms around Michael's waist. Michael grimaces in pain as his back and one of his ribs crack. He tries to strike back, or at least create a space beneath the boy's arms, but can't: the boy pulls him in all directions and picks him up. Then, with a perfectly executed back suplex, he releases Michael mid-air and sends him flying across the room. Michael's shoulders and the back of his skull absorb most of the impact, and he stands back up, banged up but still determined. The young man slaps his pecs, smiling. Michael gets back into position and tries to visualize the holds he learned as a child. "Not the legs," he whispers to himself, beholden to decorum despite the high stakes. "Not the legs, just the upper body." This time he's more aggressive. He stays low and manages to get his opponent into a headlock, which the boy responds to with a headlock of his own. A war of attrition begins as both try to sweep each other, both countering each move. Michael's every muscle strains. Sweat pours from his body. The boy manages to break free, takes Michael by the waist again and slams him to the ground with a skillful front suplex. Michael's back swells on impact. But this time the boy won't let go. The fight moves to the floor. Somewhat dazed, Michael still can't break free, powerless to stop the boy as he flips Michael over and smashes his chest against the tile floor. The boy, who is now straddling him from behind in a vaguely erotic position, squeezes Michael so hard he feels his organs compressing. Michael's legs go numb as the blood flow is all but cut off. He tries to push up on the floor with his arms so he can gain the space for a half twist and hopefully break free. An adrenaline rush gives Michael the strength to turn, but instead of a half twist, he does a complete twist; his adversary won't give an inch. The young man's technical advantage appears impossible to beat.

"Give up!" cries the boy confidently, squeezing harder. Michael's face is bright red and he's barely breathing. He can tell he's about to faint, about to see the victories of the past few hours completely nullified. For once—perhaps even for the first time in his life—he thinks, *to hell with fair play*. Grunting, he pushes up on the floor and manages to get onto all fours despite his opponent's weight on his back. Then with one quick move, he reaches for his ankle with his right hand, grabs his Epipen, and plants it in his opponent's thigh. The boy releases him and starts violently convulsing. Michael gets up, coughs, and puts him in an illegal yet effective sleeper hold. After a couple minutes of trembling and shaking, the boy lies passed out in the middle of the ring, his breathing regular. Victorious, Michael sits next to him on the cold floor, taking a minute to catch his breath. He stares at the boy. Now that he's sleeping like a baby, his youth is particularly striking, almost disturbing.

An eerie calm settles over the white house in the wake of the brutal combat. Michael struggles to his feet and grabs his bag and pistol. He's out of darts, but he can always use his gun to threaten or strike, if need be. He looks around to make sure everyone he's neutralized is still out cold, which they are. He notices a series of white marble busts on display that he's never seen before. He exits the hall and, rounding the corner, sees the two young boys who fled earlier. They are creating some sort of human shield in front of the door of the old home theater. They tense slightly at the sight of Michael's weapon pointed at them, but stay where they are.

"What's behind that door?" Michael yells at them.

They don't answer. Michael walks calmly toward the protected room, expecting an ambush.

"You saw what I did to your friends. I'm not in the mood to play games. Do yourselves a favor and answer me. Who are you? What are you doing here? What do you want from me? What's behind this door—what are you protecting? Answer me!"

The two curly-haired boys give him a defiant look and take a step forward. They puff out their chests and cross their arms. Then one of them speaks.

"Is there really a door? What is a door? What is the meaning of this door? What is meaning?"

"If there are doors," adds the second boy, "are there also non-doors?"

Furious, Michael runs at them, yelling. He's in pain, but he doesn't let on. The boys look at each other briefly, worried, but hold their positions, knees quivering slightly. The first feels one of his vertebrae snap as Michael delivers a violent blow that knocks him against the wall, while the second takes an upper-cut to the chin and collapses like a puppet. The path is clear.

The double solid-wood door is locked. Michael puts an ear up against it. He can hear something. He tries to force the handle, then bangs on the door with both fists.

"Open the door!" he cries, his voice hoarse. "Open the door! Open the door!"

He hesitates. He's seen enough movies to know that no matter how much one perseveres in such situations, there's no guarantee it will pay off. The real solution is in his bag. He pulls out a plastic explosive with an adhesive strip and sticks it near the lock, pushing in two metal rods connected to wires. They're attached to a small detonator that Michael holds in his hand. He takes a step back and frowns.

"I have a right to know," he murmurs.

He pushes the button. Splinters of wood explode in all directions and Michael momentarily loses his hearing from the deafening blast. He coughs and wipes the dust from his face. In the room, the smoke is so thick that he can't see a thing. He creeps forward, stretching his jaw to unblock his ears. He squints, still unable to see clearly. Then the smoke begins to clear. He can make out a shape. He stops dead in his tracks and gasps. Before him stands an elderly man in a toga, his back to Michael. The space, which has been converted into a large living room, contains about fifty men, all silently watching him. A moment passes. The older man slowly turns his head to the side, acknowledging Michael's presence.

"Welcome, my son."

Michael drops to his knees.

"Son?"

The man turns around. He comes up to Michael and extends his hand. Michael gets to his feet, never taking his eyes off the man's face. His features are vaguely familiar. His thick white beard and white hair. His piercing eyes. Wrinkled forehead. Wise smile. Slowly, he guides Michael to a small podium. It seems Michael is to address the assembly. Spotlights shine on him. He looks over the room, dumbfounded by what he sees. Sartre, Kant, Derrida, Heidegger, Hegel, Voltaire, Marx, Hume, Foucault, Nietzsche, and so many others, all dressed in togas, seemingly de rigueur, all with chest tattoos. In the front row, Don Simpson beams at him, his eyes filled with pride.

The bearded man speaks.

"Michael Bay, by the power vested in me, I welcome you to the Brotherhood of the World's Greatest Minds."

Simpson steps forward and gently places a laurel wreath onto Michael's head. Overwhelmed by events,

263

Michael just stands there. The room erupts into enthusi-astic applause. Amid the thunderous ovation, Michael turns to the old man, bewildered.

"Who are you?"

"You know who I am, Michael. I'm Plato."

The ancient philosopher, leather sandals on his feet, talks as they stroll through the garden. Despite a life spent in cinema, Michael can't suspend his disbelief. Has he gone mad? Has he been unknowingly drugged? All the guards he neutralized have recovered and, at the sight of the wreath, bow respectfully as he passes.

"You'll have to excuse my men for their lack of pro-fessionalism. Most are still quite young, you know. You were never supposed to see them. But their train-ing clearly did not prepare them for your keen eye on the world. I never wanted you to feel spied upon. But I needed to follow your progress. To make sure you were developing to your full potential."

"The... the photographers... that was you?"

"Don't be simplistic, Michael. They're not just photographers. They're apprentice philosophers, above all. Field philosophers. You must understand, it's diffi-cult for me to go out in public without raising suspicion. My face is in every museum. Someone would recog-nize me and discover the existence of the Brotherhood. Humanity is not yet ready. It's the same for Jean-Paul,

Emmanuel, Friedrich... So we need these young men, to whom we offer a humanistic education. They are trained in the matters of the spirit, but also the reality of the streets."

"I... I couldn't have known. I thought they were hostiles. I hurt a few of them quite badly..."

"Don't worry yourself with all that, Michael. I'm certain they'll be able to take a philosophical view of their injuries."

The night has settled. The air is cool but comfortable. The birds are silent. A few crickets rub their wings together.

"There are so many things I don't understand."

"Admitting is the first step to understanding."

"But you're dead! You're all dead! I saw Don Simpson die with my own eyes!"

"This sense of wonder is the mark of the philosopher. Our work has allowed us to reach a higher level of existence. In other words, you've just emerged from the cave, Michael. You're ready to see things other than the shadows."

"Why here, in this house? What are you doing here?"

"The house has always belonged to us. It's part of our property portfolio. Ordinarily our headquarters are close to Athens, but since you're our greatest hope in such a long time, we thought it best to relocate for a few years, to be closer, to better guide you."

"Oh... And Jim and Harriett? Do you know what happened to them, sir?"

265

"No need for the sir, Michael. You're one of us now."

Michael takes a moment to digest the fact that he's on first-name terms with Plato.

"Do you know what happened to them?"

"Their real names are Isidore and Andromache. They work with us. We don't usually deal with women, but we made an exception for this particular mission. You know... even though they knew from the start that this day would come, the pain of separation has been profound. They were extremely devoted—they're professionals—but they became attached... They never lost hope of rekindling their relationship with you. And I understand: it wasn't only the familial bond—for a long time, they had difficulty accepting that they'd alienated a future Great Mind. But the separation was necessary for you to develop. Their feelings for you were so strong that, despite our warnings, they continued to try to reach out to you. We had to send them out on another mission. They now live in Germany and are raising another one of our hopefuls. A young man by the name of Markus Gabriel. He doesn't have quite your potential, but we nonetheless believe that he could accomplish great things."

"Will I ever see them again?"

"That would be unwise, Michael. They've already grieved your loss. You must respect that. And seeing them again could compromise their cover."

Michael rubs his temples. He's tired. The world around him seems different. His disbelief slowly retreats.

"And Daphné? If I understand correctly, you were behind her kidnapping too? Why did you want to separate us so badly?"

"That woman was a distraction, Michael. There are rare exceptions, but we consider all women to be distractions. Call me conservative, but I've always seen the classic way of things as superior. We've always favored the transfer of knowledge from man to man. It worked two thousand five hundred years ago, and must still work today. I know that you had feelings for her, but you must know that she would always have kept you from spreading your wings. They don't have the necessary sensibility to comprehend the subtleties of your reflections. I admit, our initial reaction, with the kidnapping and all, was rather excessive, but we were frightened for you. For all of us."

"You... You'll have to excuse me, Plato, but this is a lot to take in. And what I just can't understand is... why me? You're inviting me into a brotherhood, putting me on the same level as Hegel and Rousseau... Yet I've tried so hard and failed to gain recognition as an intellectual! It's as though people take cruel delight in ridiculing my work. I'm continually refused institutional recognition. I'm the laughing stock of colleges. You must have the wrong person..."

"Who among us was truly appreciated when we were alive? We all came up against the hostility of our contemporaries, who, behind the façade of thinkers, only truly valued the prospect of climbing the rungs of society.

Many of our brothers were even murdered for ideas that were considered too provocative. Even recently. You saw what happened to Don... He spent his life trying to democratize critical thinking, but his opponents prevailed. The sophists eliminated Don Simpson just as they did my own mentor, Socrates. They continue to throw wrenches in our wheels."

"So it wasn't an allergic reaction?"

"No, Michael. He was poisoned. You know, in a way he gave his life for you. He appeased our opponents so you could continue your work. I don't want you to feel guilty: a true philosopher does not fear death."

"And Bruckheimer? He's not part of the Brotherhood?"

"Jerry is a good soldier, no doubt about that. But he isn't quite ready to join us. That may change after his death. You should know that you've surpassed him in our hierarchy, however."

"But why me? All the other members of the Brotherhood are dead, but I'm still alive, as far as I know... And all I'm good for is making action flicks for teenage boys."

"But, Michael, that's just it! Our goal has always been to reach young men! Your instincts are perfectly in sync with classical philosophy's modus operandi. And in terms of your early acceptance, it's true that we're not in the habit of inviting the living into our ranks, but an exceptional mind calls for exceptional measures. With just a few films, you've not only managed to broach subjects as varied as they are vital, you've also managed to do so in a perfectly appropriate form for your era. With your overly coded and exaggerated style, you refuse complacency and shake up criticism, detracting from the society of the spectacle and its superficiality, and condemning today's attention deficit with the fast cuts in your films. Not to mention the skillful system of references to philosophical history scattered throughout your work. I was particularly charmed, I must admit, by the omnipresence of street lights in your shots—an obvious nod to the philosophers of the Enlightenment."

For the first time, Michael feels as though he is fully understood.

"It's so... I don't know... This all makes sense. But at the same time, it doesn't..."

"That's just it, Michael. What is meaning? I'd like to hear your thoughts."

"Always the same question!"

"It's not just any question. It's perhaps the most important of all questions. We've invited you to join us because we believe you may have an answer. Not necessarily *the* answer, but a meaningful one nonetheless. So, Michael, in your opinion, what is meaning?"

A shadow of distress crosses Michael's face.

"I don't know... I don't know! I have a feeling that meaning is something that can't be grasped, something fleeting. As though born of an illusion. Or maybe of transformation. Yes, there... that's the right word... transformation. Every time we think we've understood, meaning transforms, evolves into something else, something different. That's the tragedy of philosophy. I believe that a philosopher's work is to represent this continual transformation through language, whether in words or pictures. To understand meaning is to understand the fundamental impossibility of understanding meaning, but it's also about never bowing to resignation, about actively contributing to the description of something that will always differ from what's being described. To be a philosopher is to courageously agree to take on a challenge that's doomed from the start. To a certain extent, philosophy itself is, and always has been, just as illusory as its object of study, a long lesson in humility hidden behind pompous vocabulary. Anyway, I'm not making much sense. But if I really have to answer, that's what I think. The mystery of meaning dwells in transformation."

Plato reflects on his protégé's answer. He nods, satisfied, then smiles.

"It seems you have the premise for at least one new film, my son. Your work has only just begun."

ON CINEMA

A HELICOPTER FLIES through the sky as day breaks on the horizon. All is calm inside the modern and impressively large white house. All the members of the Brotherhood have returned to their quarters for the night. All except Michael, who can't get to sleep.

Still overwhelmed by his meeting with the Great Minds, in whose footsteps he's always tried to follow, Michael wanders the silent house pondering his past, present, and future. He doesn't quite know how to manage the whirl of conflicting emotions. True, he has always sought the approval of intellectual authority figures, which he's just received in a most spectacular and unexpected way. True, he now knows he's understood and appreciated by the world's most elite group of thinkers. So why doesn't he feel relieved? Why can he never be satisfied with what he has? Will he ever feel truly accomplished? He doesn't feel relieved, just weary. Empty.

The house itself fills him with melancholy. Every wall and every room is a painful reminder of his greatest mistake: severing the link with Jim and Harriett. Knowing that break was no doubt necessary for his development does not, at this particular moment, ease the pain. He longs to turn back time, to do things differently. He longs to tell them he's sorry, that he loves them, that he is thankful for how they raised him to be a good person, but he knows he'll never see them again. He longs to fly to Germany so he can find them, hug them, hold them. But now, with the honor of entering the Brotherhood of the World's Great Minds, comes great responsibility, including preserving the continuity of the history of philosophy. Compromising his parents' cover would put young Markus' training at risk and undermine a mission he must now defend.

Debris still litters the floor around the door he blew to shreds several hours earlier. The room where he had been crowned is now empty. He can look around now. It bears little resemblance to the projection room it once was. An agora now fills the space where theater seats once stood, while mirrors hang in place of the movie posters that once decorated the walls. He walks the length of these walls, running his fingertips along the surface, trying to somehow reclaim the space. He stops in a corner of the room. A panel in the wall once hidden by a piece of furniture catches his attention. "Maybe..." he thinks, and crouches down, suddenly very alert. He pushes gently on the wood panel and it opens to reveal a small hiding spot. It's dark inside. Michael reaches in and finds a dusty metal box at the back, no doubt forgotten by his parents in the move. On the lid is a yellowed label. He recognizes his mother's handwriting: *73-74*. His chin trembles. "Could it be?" He pops open the lid with his thumb and his eyes instantly brim with tears. Inside the box are three reels of 8 mm film. He closes the box and hugs it against his chest. So this is where his mother had hidden her home movies.

The photographs and papers Michael had strewn across the floor of his old bedroom are still there. Without a thought to what he's stepping on, he walks quickly toward the old projector he had noticed right before he lost his temper. The projector, designed well before the age of built-in obsolescence, still seems to be in working order. Michael excitedly takes one of the reels and hastily loads it into the projector, plugging it in and turning it to face a blank wall. His movements are quick, precise, efficient. His eyes are still wet, but there's a smile on his face that's impossible to suppress, and that begins to make his jaw muscles ache. Everything is ready. He closes the door, turns off the overhead light and, in the middle of the room, now filled with the orange glow of daybreak filtering through the shutters, turns on the projector. The motor whirrs. A clicking sound adds to the suspense as he waits for the image to appear. The square of white light illuminating the wall vivifies. Images in saturated colors flicker by too quickly. Race cars cross the frame at an impressive, almost impossible speed. The shot pans to the right to a little boy jumping excitedly up and down. He's waving his arms in the air beside a racetrack. Michael recognizes himself, unsurprised but fascinated. The shot's composition is astonishingly masterful and highly dynamic. Another panorama shows Jim: smiling, eyes sparkling, clearly bursting with love for his adopted son. Through his own smile Michael lets out a sob that he stifles with his hand. On the wall, Jim says something he can't hear, walks over toward young Michael and, after tracing an enormous V on his chest with his finger, picks him up. The camera zooms in fluidly to the duo with a low-angle spinning shot as race cars tear up the track in the background. After a moment of visual confusion, the camera changes hands and Harriett appears, wraps her arms around the little boy and covers him in kisses. Sitting on his bedroom floor, surrounded by the remnants of his past, Michael is emotional yet calm, as though something inside him has just been defused.

The reels fly by, as do the hours. Michael is exhausted but happy, a state he'd thought up until recently would elude him forever. The words "Your work has only just begun" play on loop in his head. His mind gradually returns to its usual fervor. He suddenly has a thousand projects, each more urgent than the last. A cinematic adaptation of the allegory of the cave. It could be a good opportunity to work with Ewan McGregor, who is said to be well-versed in post-Socratic philosophy. And at least one film on transformation as a space for reflection on the meaning of meaning. An homage to Don Quixote in the form of a fable on the American dream in the body-building world. Maybe the time has come to start mentoring too, to cross over into producing films directed by others... Decidedly, his work has only just begun. The academic world has yet to be conquered.

Michael gazes out his bedroom window at the laurel tree in the yard as he runs his fingers along the wreath crowning his head. He thinks of Apollo, god of poetry, whose symbol is the laurel wreath. Apollo who himself fell—in vain—for an unattainable Daphné, nymph of the river who, fleeing him, is transformed into a laurel tree. He runs his fingers along the wreath and thinks to himself that, in some way, this honorary distinction forever binds him to his own Daphné, and her memory no longer pains him. He runs his fingers along the wreath and thinks in amusement of his old friend Meat Loaf, whose vision of the world as a coherent system seems to have finally prevailed.

"Your work has only just begun," he repeats, more and more convinced, his head full of projects. Inspiration is the detonator for the explosions of his mind. He looks outside and the quiet suburban morning transforms, through the lens of subjectivity, into a thrilling scene where images flash side by side: two squadrons of fighter planes, a highly trained SWAT team, sports cars of every color, fireworks, helicopters silhouetted against the setting sun, endless clouds of flames, giant robots, blazing gunfire and, as the first notes of an Aerosmith song ring out, the flag of the United States of America proudly billowing in the wind.

QC Fiction brings you the very best of a new generation of Quebec storytellers, sharing surprising, interesting novels in flawless English translation.

Available from QC Fiction:

Visit **qcfiction.com** for details and to subscribe
to a full season of QC Fiction titles.

MIX
Paper from
responsible sources
FSC® C100212

Printed by Imprimerie Gauvin
Gatineau, Québec